~

Blood Moon Chronicles

H.R. Toye

Cody Toye

Copyright©2012

Blood Moon Press

ISBN: 978-0615678504

Blood Moon Press

115 East 7th Street

Mulberry, AR 72947

I0519856

Intro

Sometimes in life, it is necessary to run face first into a brick wall. What I mean is, sometimes the pain of taking on obstacles head first is an absolute must in order to find the strength to overcome it. That is what the Blood Moon Chronicles is, a means to overcome that stubborn brick wall and come away with a little bruising but still intact.

After spending some time as a fiction writer, a small dispute had us seeking another means of getting heard. Several stories once published and once available to you, the masses, had just vanished. This sent my writing career into a downward spiral and my stories started to collect dust in the virtual basement of my laptop's memory banks. Then, a few kind words were spoken that ignited the flame once more and helped me charge said wall with a force greater than that of the very cement that held it together. This one is for you.

Atertra, Merlin, Kane, Nita, Neria, Ichi, Xion, EvilDeath, and everyone else who's world suddenly collided with my own. (you know who you are)

Table of Contents

Thorazine

H.R. Toye

5 years ago

"No, I won't do it. No, you can't make me do it. I won't, I simply won't," he shakes his head violently. He looks around the room, white; white walls, white ceiling, and white tile floor. Everything is so blaringly white, he squints his eyes to accommodate the brightness. The tremors overtake his body; he shakes so violently he fears he will come apart.

"No, no, no, no, NOOOOO!" He wails and screams. The whiteness is blinding, he slumps to the floor. Trembling, he rolls across the tile until he bumps into the wall. He thrashes trying to loosen his bonds, to no avail. Giving up on his restraints, he starts to bash his head against the wall. It has to stop, he can't stand anymore.

A sting in his arm, a burn as it travels downward. Bees! Yes, he hears the buzzing now. He has been stung and the pain is immense. "Get them away from me, please!" The swarm is buzzing all around. Again and again he is stung. Beginning to cry now, tears of pain and terror pour from his eyes.

"Rest now, this will help," the nurse pulls the needle out and exits the room. The door shuts and a bolt is slid into place.

"No, no, nooooo," the darkness overtakes him and he sleeps. He doesn't know how long he has slept; when he finally wakes, he is overtaken by images of blood. Blood runs in rivulets down the wall and pools on the floor. He begins to laugh. Shrill giggles pierce the room and echo back to him. Startled by the sound, he holds his body motionless.

He is being watched. He edges backward toward the wall. Huddled in the corner he scrutinizes the other three; satisfied there is no device which could be used to spy on him, he turns his attention to the door. The door has a small sliding window. Even though it is closed, he can see the mesh wire that covers the opening.

Someone is watching him, he knows it. Sweat dampens his temples and collects above his lip. The unseen menace is surely plotting his demise. He won't let it happen. If somebody comes for him, he'll kill them. "No, I won't" he yells to the empty room. Yes, if they come for you, you will kill them. "No," his head slumps against his chest. Tears run freely from his eyes.

10 years ago

The voices will not stop. I see blood everywhere; violent images encompass my every waking thought. At the grocery store, I approach the meat counter. I ask the butcher for some pork chops. That is when I see it. The butcher does not bring out a cut of succulent pig, no, it's an infant. The butcher brings his cleaver down on the squirming pink child; a scream is cut short as he lops off its head.

I vomit, there on the floor. It splashes on my shoes. The baby murderer is once again just a man, with cuts of pork. "Are you alright sir, can I get you some water?"

The blood splattered apron, the smell of entrails. It is too much. I clasp my hand over my mouth, trying to stop the fresh spew of bile. It comes anyway, dripping from my fingers and running down the front of my shirt.

"Sir...?" The man behind the counter questioned. I wipe my hand on my pants and make for a hasty retreat, leaving him with the task of cleaning up my mess. I walk quickly towards the aisles of canned goods. It is free of customers. I sit on the floor and begin to rock back and forth. Groceries can wait, I need to get home. Rising from the floor, I head for the front of the store. I grab a bottle of water out of the soda cooler and go to the register.

The pretty young cashier asks if I found everything alright. She tries not to notice my disheveled appearance. Suddenly her face erupts into a mass of bloody flesh. Her eyes glow and horns sprout from the top of her head. "I will kill you, you fucking piece of shit." The five dollar bill drops from my hand onto the floor. Fuck the water, I run towards the door.

"Sir, your water…"

I hit the door, hard. I feel my nose crunch and a warm stream flow from it. Drops of blood mix with the mess on my shirt; I wipe my arm across my face and leave a smear down my sleeve. I make it outside. The sunlight burns my eyes and I fumble for my sunglasses. They were bent out of shape from the fight with the door. I put them on anyway; they helped to shield my burning retinas.

Walking down the sidewalk, drips of blood continue to fall. As they splash onto the concrete they turn into spiders, fat, black spiders. I feel it pop and crunch as I squash one beneath my tennis shoe. I hate spiders.

I reach the bus stop. An old woman is sitting on the bench. As I watch she ages, her bones turn to dust beneath my gaze. "What are you gawking at, boy?" I quickly turn away, not wishing to have any further communication with the dust-that-used-to-be-human.

*****

The bus finally approaches, it looks safe enough. Climbing the three steps, I glance towards the back. Everything seems alright. Handing the bus driver my token I move about half-way down the aisle and grab a seat. I am sitting across from a pretty young mother with her sleeping toddler. Her head is leaning against the glass; I think she is asleep too.

Her arm is draped around his shoulders. They look so peaceful. A black line appears on her face. It grows and spreads like a vine, down her neck and under the sleeve of her sundress. It's climbing down her arm, the one wrapped around the boy. Tendrils of black reach from the vine-like markings towards the boy.

Wisps of blackened smoke reach for his nostrils and mouth. It is going to choke him, it will kill him. Thinking fast, I jump up and grab the boy. I have to save him! The mother wakes up and starts screaming at me, "My baby, give me my boy."

Her shrieks of rage turn to sobs as she reaches for her child. The smoke and vines disappear, leaving her a normal woman once again.

The boy is crying now too, having been startled awake by the force with which I grabbed him. I thrust the boy back into her arms and run to the front of the bus. "Driver let me off."

"Son, you need to take your seat while the bus is in motion."

"I need off, NOW!" Something about the way I sounded, or maybe looked, caused him to comply. Of course, the wailing mother and child could have been the cause as well.

*****

I walked back to my apartment; it took me nearly an hour to walk the two miles. I needed to get inside; there was too much going on for me to concentrate. I needed the familiarity of my tiny one-bedroom.

The final straw was when the neighbor's stupid cement lion that kept guard outside her door came to life and took a swipe at my leg. I ran screaming through the hallway. More than one curious neighbor opened the door to peek out through the crack that was allowed while the security chain was in use.

Once inside, with the door securely latched behind me, I collapsed onto the futon in the living room. Sweat dripped from my brow and darkened the pits of my t-shirt. I haven't been sleeping well. I tried to convince myself that was the reason I was seeing some strange shit.

I pulled off my shirt and tossed it on the floor. Next, I kicked off my shoes. I lay on the crappy excuse for a couch for a long time. I didn't watch the television or listen to music; I just stared at the ceiling. I ceased trying to figure out what was going on. "Fuck it, maybe next time I'll hallucinate a chick whose clothes fall off."

I laughed out loud at this, and then stopped when I noticed it didn't quite sound sane. Maybe someone slipped me something. I scoffed at this; I hadn't had any company in over a month. I haven't wanted to see anybody, so no one could have secretly given me a drug.

Things have been going downhill for me. I missed too many days at work and got fired; I'm living off of the money I had been saving back to buy a car outright. I almost had enough too; eventually it's going to run out. Then what? Cut my fucking throat and rid the world of Ezra Plum. "I can see it now, my gravestone will read 'Here lies Ezra Plum, he was a peach of a man' no wait, 'He was a sour grape.'"

I had been hearing fruit jokes my entire life, maybe they finally warped me. I laughed until tears sprang from my eyes and my jaws ached. When I had regained some measure of control, I turned my face to the back of the couch. I snuggled with the throw pillow, and at last got some sleep.

*****

When I woke up, the room was dark. Someone is whispering my name, again and again. I lie very still on the futon, trying to determine where the voice is coming from. Someone must have broken in; did I leave the door unlocked?

I slowly move my eyes, trying not to draw attention to myself. Certainly they know I am here, who else would be calling my name but the intruder? I've had enough; I refuse to play games with the burglar. If they are going to kill me, so be it. I refuse to die a coward trying to melt into my couch.

I jump up and scream at the top of my lungs, "Who's there, what do you want?" I can't see anyone, the room isn't that dark. Surely if someone was here, I could see them. The apartment has an open floor plan, I can clearly see into the kitchen from my position in front of the futon.

Only two rooms are not visible, the bedroom and the bathroom. If someone was hiding, it would have to be in either of those rooms. Luckily they are both leading off the kitchen, so I can grab a weapon before checking them out. I walk quietly into the kitchen and grab a knife from the block on the counter.

It was only as I was pushing open the bathroom door, that I noticed my weapon of choice: a paring knife. Well, at least it's sharp. My left hand snakes into the room and flips the light switch. My plan was to blind the intruder and surprise him with a stab wound. That was my plan, until the sudden illumination caused my eyes to burn and water. I was rendered helpless until my vision adjusted.

When my eyes focused, I could see that no criminal lurked in the bathroom. Tired of sneaking about I barged into the bedroom yelling wildly. That would shock the intruder and allow me enough time to attack before he or she could regain their composure. Seeing the figure hiding in the corner I lunged, paring knife first.

I stabbed repeatedly where I thought I could do the most damage, right in the… sock? I brought the knife close to my face and saw the tube sock dangling from the blade. I had just viciously attacked my pile of dirty laundry. I stood upright and clicked on the lamp beside my bed. The room stood empty. I was alone in my apartment.

My stomach growled reminding me it had not had food in quite some time. In truth, I can't remember the last time I ate. I went to the kitchen and tossed my weapon in the sink. Opening the fridge, I was reminded why I had gone to the grocery store earlier today. Little more than condiments remained inside. I picked up a half empty jar of grape jelly. A PB&J sounded like just the thing to shut my stomach up. Grabbing the loaf of bread and peanut butter, I set about making my paltry meal.

I eat standing over the sink, a mindless task. I take no pleasure in the sandwich, it is just a means to keep my stomach quiet and fuel my body. Sitting on the couch I reach for the pack of smokes from the coffee table. I struck a match. The flame enthralled me. The fire melted and reformed. It dripped down the sides of the wooden stick to the edge of my fingers. Then, sudden searing pain. "Son of a bitch!" Dropping the match, I sucked on the blister forming on my left index finger.

The smell of burning carpet fibers forced me to act quickly. I grabbed my discarded shirt and smothered the flame. I need to be more careful. I quickly struck another match and stuck it to the tip of my cigarette. I shook the fire out before I could become entranced once again. I inhaled deeply, allowing the smoke to fill my lungs. I finished the cigarette quickly and crushed the butt out in the ashtray.

Pacing the small living room, I realized I was restless. What had once seemed a cozy apartment now seemed confining. I needed to get out. I quickly returned to my room and grabbed a fresh shirt. I went back to the living room and slipped on my shoes. I grabbed my keys from the coffee table and stuffed them into my pocket. Locking the door behind me, I went for a walk.

*****

Full darkness had blanketed the city. I didn't care. I had to go somewhere. I don't know how long I was walking when I happened upon the park. The bench was positioned under the florescent glow of a street lamp at the edge of the recreational area. My feet hurt and my body is weary, so I sit down to rest.

My eyes were closed; perhaps I dozed off for a bit when I was startled by the giggling. Two teenage girls where looking in my direction and whispering. Was I snoring? What were they doing here so late anyway, I grumbled to myself. They brazenly moved closer to me. Probably daring each other to talk to me.

As they approached, their bodies began to shift. Pustules appeared on their faces. The smell of rot encompassed them. Gaping holes riddled their skin and bits of flesh began to drop from their bodies. Thin, elongated arms reached for me. Frozen with fear, I screamed. I had no weapon, nothing to defend myself.

I couldn't simply sit there and wait for them to claim me for their unholy purpose. I had to act. I jumped up and ran full force towards the one on the right. My body weight toppled us both to the ground. I pummeled her with my fists. The one on the left got away, but I had this one. I would not let her wreak havoc on unsuspecting people.

I grabbed her wrists and did the only thing I could. Trying not to gag on the stench of her rotting flesh, I bent my head to her neck. My teeth sank into her throat and I kept biting. Even as she ceased struggling and I felt the hot spray of her blood drench my face, I bit. The smell of feces reached my nostrils where she had emptied her bowels when she died, but still I bit.

The one that got away, that was my mistake. Her henchmen garbed in blue returned for me. They threw me into a room. The white room as I had come to call it. I knew I was going to die there.

*****

Present day

"That is what I remember of the days leading up to my institutionalization. I was very sick. I was soon diagnosed with schizophrenia and began taking medication. I take my meds every day and have not had a hallucination since my medicine was changed five years ago. I am very sorry for killing that poor girl."

The five men and my doctor conferred for several minutes. One of them stood and told me that they believe that I have been fully rehabilitated and that I have a court order to continue taking my meds and go to therapy once a week. After ten years I am going to be released.

I return to my room and gather my things. I can take a bus downtown where I will be able to stay with my mother until an opening in a group home becomes available. In a couple of years they think I will become a fully functional member of society once again.

*****

The sun is bright and it hurts my eyes. I carry my small duffel bag of personal effects that I have acquired over the years. It's only a couple of blocks to the bus stop. I take my time walking there. The sounds of the city are something I haven't heard much of in a long time.

I look down and notice a lonely dandelion growing from a crack in the side walk. It turns black and withers under my gaze. A frown creases my brow at the sight. "Ezra, Ezra…" My name is chanted in the wind. A light rain begins to fall. My clothes and skin are streaked with red where the drops touch me.

I look up at the sky. Blood is pouring from the black clouds. I fall to my knees. A mewling sound reaches my ears from far off. It turns into wails of terror. I was less than a block from the bus stop.

Mother

Cody Toye

He watched through the frosted glass of his living room as the large snowflakes blanketed the ground on the quiet December day. They slowly danced before his window, mocking him, before snuggling next to each other just outside of his house. Just like last year and the year before, the cursed holiday brought forth a fake sense of happiness. The warm glow of his fire-place and the steam rising from his coffee cup was the only visitors he wanted this year.

Jacob took a slow sip from the hot liquid that swirled in his coffee cup. Laughter filled the air, as many of the towns children ran through the pristine hillside kicking up powder. With each step their pace slowed as their winter boots sank deeper and deeper into the holiday cheer. A smile that seemed to radiate straight from his heart started to show on his haggard face. Christmas Eve, I can allow myself a little enjoyment. After all, tomorrow will be the day that children see their family, not today. He thought to himself as he closed his eyes.

Wonderful visions danced behind his eyelids. Visions of children opening presents and getting everything they ever wished for. Parents hugged them close to their bodies in a warm embrace, cherishing the moment. Distant relatives handed obscure presents out in hopes that their many hours of indecisiveness would reap a little happiness in the kiddos. He could picture a holiday feast, filled with laughter as the new puppy that little Johnny got for Christmas begs for scraps in the most adorable fashion.

Jacob opened his eyes and inhaled deeply, letting his lungs expand fully before letting the stagnant air escape. Oh how he longed for a Christmas like that, one where he is loved and happiness is just a box away. He finished his coffee in a large gulp and chunks the cup into the fireplace. A loud crash rings out as it explodes into many bits of ceramic shards. He can feel his fury building deep inside himself.

No. I hate those kids! Why do they deserve to be happy on Christmas? What did I do different that forced Santa to kick me in the ribs instead of giving me gifts? A resigned sigh escaped. I guess it's because of her. It's because of mother that I hate Christmas. Jacob thinks about his eighth family holiday and how when no one showed up his mother got furious. They avoided her like a plague. He remembered. They knew how she was when she drank and she always drank. Sometimes she would start at three in the morning, not quitting until her limp body was found in a drunken slumber somewhere. When she would wake up, she would simply force the beer back to her lips.

That particular Christmas was when I truly knew something was wrong with her. All the other kids were getting new bicycles and a ton of presents. Their trees shined brightly with every type of glitter and lighting, illuminating the happy expressions on their faces. My mother on the other hand, spent her money making sure she would not run out of alcohol. After all, she had mentioned how badly it sucked for the stores to stay closed until the 26th. Our tree was made of a horrible smelling plastic, and had only a hand- made aluminum star on the top. Underneath was a single present addressed to Jacob, love Mom.

By the time I got to open it, I felt the tears swell up as I seen the two dollar container of army men from the Dollar Saver. I tried to be polite and thank her, but the alcohol knew I was upset. A cigarette still hung from her lips when she spoke. Her anger raised the volume of her voice as she scolded me over and over.

"ANY OTHER KID WOULD BE LUCKY TO HAVE A PRESENT LIKE THAT, BUT YOU ARE A SPOILED LITTLE BRAT! DO YOU HEAR ME JACOB? SPOILED LITTLE BRAT."

I watched her stumble to the oven, almost knocking over the tree in the process. With her beer still in one hand, she grabs the oven mitt and pulls the undercooked turkey from the oven. Mumbling something under her breath, she walks through the living room and to the doorway. I watch in horror as she opens the front door and chunks the turkey out into the snow.

"SEE WHAT BEING UNGRATEFUL GETS YOU. NOTHING. I HOPE YOU STARVE, WORTHLESS BRAT!"

Tears start free falling from my eyes and guttural sounds escape my throat as I feel the sting of mother's words. Before I knew what was happening, she snatched me by the shirt and threw me to the sofa. My eyes widened with the physical abuse, not knowing what to say or do I simply stammered.

"I-I-I'M SORRY MOMMA!"

He looked out the window once more, watching the kids throw snowballs back and forth. Some had built little forts, apparently impenetrable to all common variety snow weapons. Jacob couldn't help but wonder what all he had missed in his youth because of his mother's disease.

The disappointment was a sort of holiday tradition growing up, though mother's temper seemed to get worse every year. By the time he was an adult, she was completely out of control. Twelve packs turned to twenty fours and happy hours seemed to be from noon to midnight. Jacob tried to maintain a relationship with her, but only from a distant. Once a year, he would invite her into his life to celebrate Christmas with him...her only son. He tried so hard to make it work, putting her before his own needs. This worked for awhile. She remained civil towards his girlfriend and even managed a smile or two.

Then, on the Christmas of his twenty first year of living hell, mother decided to come down for a long holiday. A celebration of her only son's first year as a married man. Oh how he loved Jenny, so sweet and pretty. A far cry from everything his mother was. He planned on spending the rest of his life with her, eventually growing old and then being buried with matching headstones next to his beloved. To that extent, he also believed that Jenny reciprocated those feelings. But it only took three days with his mother to change her mind.

She had no sooner unpacked her suitcase, when she broke into the case of beer she brought along for the ride. After all, it's Christmas! To her, this fact alone simply meant she could drink as much as she wanted as fast as she wanted and be justified in doing so. Jenny and Jacob were snuggled next to the fireplace, sipping champagne and chuckling among each other, oblivious of what would happen to their first and only holiday together. The large pine tree, glowing as bright as the North Star on a clear summer night, contained colorful presents of every shape and size. Jenny had even bought his mother one of them fancy red hats, you know the ones, and they come with a large bow and an even larger price tag. It was her attempt to get in good with her mother-in-law, hoping for a warm welcome into the family. Everything was so perfect.

After about three hours of indulging, Mother came stumbling into the living room, bumping the mantle and shattering Jenny's favorite vase. I was appalled! Instead of "I'm so sorry" she simply flopped down on the recliner and took another swig of beer.

"That was the ugliest damn thing I ever saw, good riddance if you ask me"

"Mother! That's not very nice."

Her blood-shot eyes radiated glossy overtones; Jacob knew he was in for a rough time. Jenny started sobbing uncontrollably at the sight of her vase being turned into a makeshift jig-saw puzzle. Large fat tears streamed down her pretty face, leaving a river of mascara in its wake.

"What are you crying for darlin? Are you a big baby? Boo-Hoo, Boo-Hoo, I knew my son would marry someone as weak as he is. Careful honey, I wouldn't want you to get a splinter cleaning up that mess."

Jenny simply continued to sob quietly, and started to sweep up her family heirloom. In hopes of saving their first holiday together, not a word was said between the two. Mother continued to push buttons, showing love in the only way she knew how, through humiliation. Between the embarrassing stories of how Jacob wet the bed, to calling Jenny every name in the book, Christmas was ruined. After taking the abuse for quite some time, Jacob's sweet wife finally put her foot down.

"YOU ARE A MONSTER! HOW CAN YOU BE SO MEAN TO YOUR ONLY SON?"

"A monster? I will show you a monster darling!" she said through slurred English

It was then that mother, walked over to the tree and smashed all of the presents. She took special care to kick through the one addressed to her. After all, who would want a present from a tramp? She reminded Jenny. The next two days were spent watching her get trashed and continue her rampage. By the afternoon of the third day, Jenny had enough. She gave Jacob the choice, either mother leaves or she leaves. How could he through his own mother out, knowing she was too drunk to drive? What kind of a son would do such a thing? So it went that Jacob went through his very first divorce thanks to family roots.

Things pretty much stayed the same through the years, going through three marriages, two houses, and a dog named fluffy. Jacob had to remind himself that he only had one mother. The years came and went, seeing mother only during the holidays. He tried to be a good son, but he resented her and couldn't take more than a few hours at a time. Then about three years ago, Jacob received a call from mother saying this would be her last Christmas. She claimed to have liver cancer and would be passing soon. Passing soon? Jacob seriously doubted that. She was way to mean to die. Hell, she would probably make the Grim Reaper cry. But Jacob indulged her anyways and flew to her home for a long holiday vacation.

He no sooner arrived, when he was greeted with the wonderful smell of cooked turkey. The entire kitchen seemed to be flowing with pleasant odors. For once, his mother stayed sober long enough to cook a Christmas dinner. Jacob was feeling pretty good about his decision to come out for the weekend. Maybe mother finally got her act together. He thought to himself. Maybe we can have an actual relationship now. After a wonderful meal, he noticed his mother sneaking into the kitchen and downing a beer with only a few breathes between gulps. She was trying so hard to conceal her drinking, trying to make things right. The demons she fought had finally won though, as she finished her twelfth "secret" beer things started to go sour.

She called Jacob every name in the book and told him how bad of a failure he was. He couldn't even get a woman to stay with him. His job sucked, he sucked, his choices sucked, and he was a spoiled brat. That last sentence brought repressed memories to the surface at a most heinous time. He finally stood up to his mother, telling her what mental scars her years of abuse had caused.

The screaming matches lasted for the entire weekend, neither one surrendering to the other. Stubbornness, I wonder who I got that from? He thought to himself. His mother even went around shattering every picture she had of him, hoping to offend. Jacob just laughed at her, after all, only a drunk would think that destroying her own items would hurt others. Finally, Jacob simply gave up. He calmly packed his bags and threw on his warmest winter coat. With sad eyes he calmly turned to face his mother.

"I've had enough mother. I can't do it anymore. Stay away from me, don't call me, I hope I never see you again."

"You will honey. I will show up when you least expect it. I will be there to meet your new wife, to see your new house, even to meet your new boss. I will be there. You can't get rid of me...I'm your mother."

Jacob walked through the door and out into the cold December day, never looking over his shoulder as he walked out on her. That was the last time he had seen her. Every Christmas since, he put out his one present and put up his tree, waiting for her to come. This year was no different. He seemed to have gained some sense of self-respect over the last twelve months and expected her to swoop in and take it away. Like a plague, she would be there when he least expected it.

He stood, walking slowly to the fireplace poking the logs with a long metal fire poker. Outside he could still hear the kids laughing. A few times, he even heard a loud splat as a snow ball collided with the side of his house. He wasn't mad though, how could he be? Kids will be kids after all.

Most of them are just little bundles of happiness and who was he to damper their holiday?

He inhaled deeply and let out a defeated sigh. I don't hate them. He admitted. I envy them. They will have a wonderful holiday, just like every year and grow to be healthy adjusted adults. I on the other hand, will continue to have baggage. Emotional and mental baggage that is far too heavy for me to carry. It will continue to ruin my relationships until I die alone. Thanks mother!

Jacob stares at the Christmas tree that repeatedly blinked a false sense of happiness. Underneath it sat one neatly wrapped present, complete with an adorably over-sized bow. Why do I do this to myself? Why am I waiting for mother to show up and ruin my holiday? Why? Because I am a good son...that's why. He can feel the anger rise inside once more, a feeling that mixes heartburn and teeth chattering.

"Enough! I will open it when I damn well please! Do you hear me mother? When I want to open it I will! I don't need to wait on you." His voice echoed off of the walls rattled his eardrums. He drops to his knees and as a final act of defiance, he rips open the present. Inside sat a large object with a newspaper wrapped around it. He carefully removes it, hoping to see what it is concealing within its print.

The headline on the newspaper sends him into shivers, catching his attention like a deer in headlights. He unfolds it and holds it closer to his eyes to read. It was dated back three years exactly.

Woman killed in tragic house-fire

Doreen Smith, 62, was killed in a tragic house-fire yesterday at 1642 Lincoln Avenue. Though the cause was Arson, the suspect is unknown. According to those who knew Doreen, She was a recluse and never had company. Her only family is her son, Jacob Smith, who lost contact with her years ago...

His heart skipped a beat as he dropped the paper, spilling his mother's urn. Her ashes soaked deep into the carpet, turning it a murky brown color. In a flash, visions of the past came back to haunt him. Jacob remembered burning his mother with lighter fluid and a match while she lay passed out in a drunken stooper. He trailed the fluid all across the house, hoping to block any escape she may attempt. An accident, yes, it will look like an accident. It all became clear to him now; it came back as it really happened. After the first night of arguing, he killed his mother in her sleep and slipped out in the middle of the night.

He repressed the memory, wrapping all evidence of its existence into a fancy little present to be opened only on Christmas. Jacob smiled as he scooped the remaining ashes back into its fancy home. He wrapped it back up with the news article and placed it back in its box. As he turned to grab the vacuum from the closet it, a thought occurred to him. Mother had won. She will always be there to ruin Christmas.

Clone

Cody Toye

His favorite spot moaned and creaked from his weight. A nice hollowed-out imprint of his ass adorned the broken down brown loveseat. It has been three weeks since he left his house for more than a quick jaunt to the liquor store. A stack of past due bills littered the floor near a box of moldy pizza. Chad shook his head in disgust. Not from the condition in which he has been living, but rather from seeing his favorite football team losing once again. Life is just unfair.

The orange smudgy finger prints left ugly little streaks as he wiped them across the denim of his jeans. With little effort, he wadded up the empty bag of chips and tossed them casually towards the trash heap in the corner in an attempt to appease the rats. Depression sank in, and once again, he remembered where he was.

Another job came and went. This time it wasn't his fault. It was never his fault. The supervisors always seemed to pick on him, the hours were always wrong, and the job was always too hard. A large sigh escaped in a wheezy fashion as he lights another cigarette and slides his hand across the mess on the loveseat. Stacks of papers and day old food particles came crashing down to their final resting place upon the floor.

Channel after channel, he surfed the high waves of cable television before returning to the football game. He stands and stretches, slowly walking across the weak floor of his trailer house. The smell of spoiled milk and rotted meat fills the air as he opens the fridge and selects a beer. After settling down in his favorite butt groove, something catches his eye. Video footage from a liquor store robbery flashes before the screen. He knows that place; it's the one right around the corner. I was just there last night, he thinks to himself while watching the news bulletin.

The newscaster straightens his tie and solemnly stares into the camera. "This just in…at seven pm Bob's Liquor Emporium was robbed at gunpoint. The suspect is still at large. He is six foot one and weighs one hundred and eighty pounds. He has brown hair and green eyes. He also has a tattoo of a snake on his right arm and is considered armed and extremely dangerous." The following video shows the assailant coming into the store. If you have any information please call law enforcement immediately!

Chad snickered to himself as he stared at the cobra coiled around his right bicep. I guess I should turn myself in he thought. The resemblance was amazing. They have my description down to a T. A spray of beer came flooding from his mouth as he watched the footage. It was me! How is that possible? Sirens blared in the distance, echoing through the silent summer day. Louder and louder they roared until they were rolling down the main entrance into the trailer park.

Panic and confusion engulfed him. The loud clank of the glass being knocked over did not concern him. He scrambled around the mess looking for his sneakers. His sneakers and his tank top were snatched up in a frenzy and placed upon his lanky body. He ran towards the blinds, trying to make sense of the madness that invaded his world. Sunlight poked its warm face through the blinds in tiny slivers making his pupils contract in protest. Once adjusted, he could see two officers crawling out of their cruisers. Hands on their side-arms, they strolled up the driveway towards his front door.

He grimaced at the thought of being shot in his own living room. As they approached the thick aluminum door, dressed in perfect police attire, his legs began to tremble. The terrible two were complete carbon copies of himself. The loud thud on the door broke the shocked trance that held him. He sprinted as fast as he could through the backdoor of his home.

The two Officer Chads kicked in the door just in time to watch his sneakers blur out the back. They walked, steady and strong, through the muck inside the trailer house. Their pistols aimed high as they made their way out the back door and into the warm day. They weren't here to arrest him. They were here to kill him. Chad ran through the yards, jumping fences and dodging branches. His body ached and his lungs were threatening strike, but still he ran.

He made it to Mrs. Jenkins house when he decided to take a breather. His chest expanded and settled in large heaves trying to regain the steady pace of his heartbeat. He stared through the path he had just carved to see if they were hot on his tail. With no officers in sight, he leaned against the large oak tree and struck a match. The smoke swirled deep as his first drag on the cigarette helped settle his nerves. Making sense out of all of this seemed like an improbability. For now, he thought, I will have to keep three steps ahead of...um...myself.

Fear reared its ugly head once again as he saw Mrs. Jenkins staring out the window at him. The bright yellow of her favorite sundress gave her away. She was baking an apple pie, filling the country air with a delicious scent. However, this time it was another duplicate baking the pie.

What am I going to do? Where am I going to go? Chad felt very alone as he leaned against the tree. He yearned for something…anything that would bring some sanity into all of this. His thoughts were interrupted by a familiar sound. A loud purring came from beneath his legs. Back and forth the gentle rub of Fitzgerald, Mrs. Jenkins cat, soothed him.

"Good kitty, who's a good kitty? Chad blindly stroked the cat's fur again and again. His hand stumbled upon a nasty bald spot on the head of the loveable pet. "Who's a good kitty?" To his surprise, a loud familiar voice came booming out of the cat.

"I am. I'm a good kitty!" Looking down upon the face of the Chad kitty brought out his survival instincts. With a hard kick, the mutant cat went flying high into the air. Chad ran, deeper and deeper, through the pastures letting the swarm of confusion loose on his already fragile mind.

*****

The tall grass felt horribly itchy on his exposed legs. He could feel his pursuers gaining on him. Visions of the horrific things to come help him keep pace. The more his heart struggled in protest, the harder he pumped his legs. After twenty agonizing minutes, the white wooden fence surrounding the highway crept into sight.

Chad leaped the white wooden fence in one swift graceful movement. Old shows on the Discovery Channel flashed in his mind. The lion closes in on the gazelle, only to be beaten by the graceful leap of the magnificent creature. He hopes he will continue the path of the gazelle and not become a tender morsel for the lions.

The clunking of his shoes against the blacktop kept steady rhythm in his ears. Any other day, many atrocities of clunky automobiles would litter the highway. Today, however, luck was not on his side. The breeze kissed his face as he ran. Sweat poured into his eyes blurring his vision. The sting and the taste of salt helped him realize his goal of survival.

More echoes broke the silence he so enjoyed. By the sounds of it, fifty or more clones were only a hundred yards behind him. The city was a grueling five miles away. Can I run five miles? What is five miles minus a pack of cigarettes a day? Why didn't I pay attention in math? His conundrum was interrupted by the sound of an old pickup truck barreling down the road. Chad watched as his velocity decreased. He grabbed the door handle and leaped up into the cab, finally looking behind him.

A hundred or more clones were still heading up the road with super human ability.

"Where are you headed buddy?"

The familiar voice brought his attention to the cab of the beat up truck. His hand clasped the cold metal of door handle, frantically working it back and forth. The lock sank deep into the frame hiding itself from the world. Chad looked around, desperate for an escape route. With renewed enthusiasm, he twirled the crank to the window. A small yelp of desperation clogged his throat as he felt it snap from the door. Still holding it in his hand, he threw the mangled metal at the clone. He watched as it bounce off of his forehead and come to a sliding halt near the floorboards.

The truck slid sideways, leaving a long nasty black streak upon the pavement. Chad's body bounced off of the windshield with a heavy thud before crashing upon the seat.

"That really hurt you shithead!"

"What do you want from me?"

The carbon copy leaned in close to whisper in his ear, leaving a pungent smell burning his nostrils.

"Who are you? Why do you look like me?" Chad could feel the panicked squeal in his voice when he spoke.

He leaned in to hear what the driver was whispering, hoping for answers.

"This is going to hurt."

"What was that? I can't hear you"

"This is gonna hurt." He whispered in inaudible tones.

"One more time, I can't hear you. What do you want from me?"

"THIS IS GOING TO HURT!" he yelled as he grabbed the back of Chad's head and bounced it off of the passenger side window.

He could feel the blood trickle from the wound. His vision was clouding and consciousness threatened to fade. The loud boom of the window and the rain of glass upon the pavement seemed surreal.

The mob finally caught up with them, running frantically towards the truck. Some avoided the glass; others refuse to acknowledge its existence. Chad could feel the truck rock back and forth as they attempted to tip the heavy vehicle. He grabbed the corners of the window and forcefully pulled. His body made it halfway, when the driver seized his leg and weighted him down.

"Where are you going? The fun is just beginning?"

In his blind panic, Chad forgot about his other leg. He thrust it forward with all of his might catching the driver square in the nose. With one final hard rocking motion, the truck tipped upon its driver side and slowly slid off into the ditch. Chad held on to the window, hoisting himself up and on the top of the door.

They climbed by the dozens after him, just for a chance to prove they were the real Chad. Many made it, only to be knocked in the head by a vicious blow from his foot. He watched them bounce and roll onto the blacktop only to get up once more. His options were limited and they were closing in fast. If I'm going to do something, now is the time. He thought

He leaped over the clones on the driver side and landed hard on his right shoulder in the grass. He felt it grind and pop, sure he dislocated it. The pain was blinding. He scrambled to his feet and took off down the highway with the herd only a few paces behind him.

He could see the large buildings proudly elevated above the landscape. The sun was reflecting the shiny windows and the traffic was non-stop. Two more miles, I can do it! His head hurt and his shoulder throbbed, He strained for oxygen as his lungs refused to expand. "Please! Please let me make it. If I survive this I will quit smoking. Anything you want, just please let me make it!" It startled him to realize the truth of the situation. He could die!

*****

Chad felt relief wash over him as he stood at the busy intersection at 32nd and Main Street. Cars, Trucks, and Vans waited impatiently for the light to turn green. The smog and the sound of road rage filled the day. This was it, he was safe. He could still hear the clones galloping in hoards close behind him, but was sure nothing could happen here.

Surely, people would notice something odd if I was attacked…right? He questioned himself. He followed the sidewalk down to Jackson Street to the right of 32nd, a small spit of a road containing only a few houses. Traffic was usually pretty slow and crossing should not be a problem, but today was somehow different. Traffic was very heavy, almost worse than Main Street. Confusion sank in as he watched many vehicles turn and slow way down. A feeling of dread crippled him.

He turned around and ran back to the intersection, hoping to avoid whatever it was that was drawing their attention down Jackson Street. What he seen didn't reach his brain with ease. So foreign a sight, the improbability of it made it into nothing more than a delusion. He looked again, and panicked. Traffic had completely stopped. Two miles of turn signals blinked repeatedly, and the turn lanes were crammed so tight, not even a quarter could squeeze between the bumpers. The oncoming lanes were clear. So clear in fact, that Chad could walk down the middle of the road and have nothing to worry about.

He ran through the turn lane, jumping over the hoods of the stationary vehicles. As his footsteps beat against the sidewalk, the loud metallic sounds of car doors became apparent. The blinking of the turn signals faded away and traffic reversed. Everyone stuck turning left abandoned their transportation to pursue on foot. A fresh wave of clones now hungered for him. A new awareness of his own mortality drove him. He watched the new wave of clones collide with the old, washing the numbers into thousands.

His shoulder hurt, his legs trembled, and his lungs were failing him. He struggled to keep pace, but had nothing left to give. He felt himself slow to a crawl, until he was merely walking fast. In the distance he could see the dam, a monument of his time in the city. Memories of the past came in a flash. He could remember the mall, where he spent all of his allowance on music. He would eat in the food court, and run into old flames. The best times of his life were spent there! He stared at the rubble scattered along the blacktop. Construction equipment, twisted metal, and splintered wood was all that remained of his past. The dam stood proud in the background, but his childhood was knocked down in the name of progress. The wrecking ball gleamed in the sunlight.

The construction clones threw down their hard hats and made a running line towards him. Outnumbered and cornered, Chad could only revel in memories of the past. This was it…he was done for. He closed his eyes and took a deep breath. He knew he wouldn't make it through this alive, but neither would they. He muscled through the crowd and hopped upon the mammoth wrecking machine. He pulled the levers and twisted the cab, propelling the large ball towards the dam. It slammed into the concrete with a thunderous boom, making a crack slowly crawl from the top to the bottom. Little bits of rubble rained down onto his old stomping ground. He was scared.

The machine shook back and forth as they attempted to drag his injured body from the cushioned seat. He slammed the ball into the dam once more, widening the crack. Large streams of water started seeping through, threatening to break. Chad kicked and screamed, thrashing wildly at his opponents. With a moment of freedom he hopped down and mustarded the strength to run towards the rapidly breaking dam. The cool water trickled down his back, his reward for the nightmare he has suffered. The swarm of clones closed in on him, leaving him defenseless. In the background, the deafening sound of his demise rang in his ears. A wide smile spread across his face as he sat down where he stood and lit a cigarette. "Come and get me you Bastards!"

Intangible Series

Note to the Readers

The Proposition started as my first bio-fi story. It was then that I fell in love with the characters and found the storyline to be too good to stay short stories. What followed was a collaboration with a manga artist and the promise to make the series into graphic novels. Just like the brick wall at the beginning of this book, I have also ran into a hard spot with these as well. My artist quit on me halfway through the first story, leaving me to find someone to replace her. Here is the first two stories in the series. With any luck the entire series will be re-released as graphic novels. Enjoy!

Intangible: The Proposition

Cody Toye

"Hate has always been an intangible force. You can't touch it, you can't smell it, and you can't control it. It has no power. Some abused the feeling with vile acts upon humanity, but it was the act itself that spread terror. Twenty years ago this was true. We brought this upon ourselves." Max adjusted himself in his horribly uncomfortable plastic chair. The clinking metal balls of the Newton's Cradle connecting back and forth did nothing to soothe him. He watched as one was struck and another moved. "You know what I don't get Doc? How you can have such a nice office, but such lousy seating."

"That's because my guests are not supposed to be comfortable, you know this Max." Max closed his eyes and imagined a plush brown recliner with a nice little cup holder and a Diet Pepsi. Doctor Blitz watched in amazement as his blue plastic chair melted and reformed into new furniture. No evidence was left behind of what was. "That was very clever Max. Now can we get back to our discussion?"

"Discussion? Cut the bullshit Doc. Why have you asked me here again? I have passed every test, answered every question, I even played by the rules for the last decade and stayed in my cell. What exactly do you want from me?" Max shot Dr. Blitz a hateful stare.

He watched as Max grew irritable. This was not good, not good at all! He stared at the lanky man and let his eyes trace the deep grooves of the nasty scar on his chin. He then shifted his attention to his eyes which constantly changed color. Behind Max were broken plaques from M.I.T. and Harvard, along with a torn picture of his family. How did it come to this? He thought to himself. Humans were always at war with each other, but it was nothing new and nothing we couldn't handle. Now we are on the brink of a catastrophe. A deep sigh was audible in the eerie silence.

"So let's have it Doc. What is the question?

The clinking of the metal spheres on his desk slowed way down. When the last one hit, they turned into little wooden puppets and danced gracefully for his amusement.

"STOP THAT!"

"What's got your panties in a bunch Doc?"

"You do! You and all of your kind."

"Easy Doc…I would hate to see what you look like inside out." A creepy smile spread across

Max's face. It seemed like an evil mocking smile that dared him to say more.

"I'm sorry Max."

"That's more like it Doc. Now then, what did you want to ask me?"

The doctor wiped the sweat from his brow and stared intently into his blue eyes. Wait. Blue eyes? Did they shift once more?

"Were you the first?"

"Why do you insist on asking questions you know the answer to? Of course I was the first. My mother tried to warn you, but you had her locked up." Max started playing with the little dancing men, giving them new moves for his entertainment. They kicked their legs and placed their hands on their hips. "Look Doc, Lord of the Dance."

"Can we focus here Max?"

"Of course."

"Do you know how we stopped more from coming? The newborns had no belly-buttons. They didn't need them. Humans feed through an umbilical cord, but your kind feeds off of emotions. We executed every infant without a belly-button. Brutal, but necessary."

"It didn't help though, did it Doc? If it did you wouldn't have invited me here today."

He knew his moment was near. Dr. Blitz despised needing his help. He slid the folder across the executive desk, spilling out a black and white photo. A man with slicked back black hair held a cup of coffee. His suit was impeccable, not a single wrinkle. In the background was a counter and a rather petite cashier wearing an apron.

"This is William. After getting a cup of coffee on the corner of 23rd and Broadway, he got angry with the cashier." The good Doctor slid another photo across to Max. An espresso machine dripped with blood. Inside the grill were large tufts of hair and an unidentifiable human head. The eyes were missing.

"After arguing with the cashier, he took it upon himself to make the machine come alive and decapitate her. The problem is, he can do anything he wants. He merely just imagines it and it happens. There is nothing we can do about it. If we arrest him, he will simply escape. If we kill him, we could start a war with...well...your kind."

Max stared at the photo uninterested. He handed it back to Dr. Blitz, burning the edges. "Great story Doc, but what does this have to do with me?"

"The government asked for your help Max. When you are the only one of your kind left, we will give you full benefits."

His eyes turned from blue to green in an instant. He narrowed his eyes into tiny slits and stared into Dr. Blitz.

"What kind of benefits?"

"To start with, you will finally have a Social Security number. We will allow you to have a job, a house, to vote, you name it. You will become a citizen of the United States. That also means no more cameras or cells. That is what you want, isn't it Max?"

"Deal."

Max held his hand out to shake, but the good doctor avoided it like the plague.

"He lives in Seattle; be prepared for a battle Max. He doesn't believe in right or wrong."

"I better get started then, huh Doc?"

Max stood, melting the recliner into the horrible plastic sadist stool that originally seated him. Happy thoughts replaced his sour mood. I will finally become a citizen. He thought of the tasks that awaited him. Nothing will stand in my way!

*****

William walked along the sidewalk taking in the warm sunshine. Every tenth crack or so, he stomped on it and imagined another pedestrian dying. Right on cue, the lady in the jogging suit clamps her chest and dies of a heart attack; he smiles and keeps walking. What a fun game, he thinks to himself. After about half an hour, he reaches his destination. Hundreds of people wait in line to buy their tickets to the wildly popular rock band, Inconsiderate Roach.

William stared at a woman in her early twenties. She wore a spiked collar and black makeup covered her face. She had the brightest blue eyes he had ever seen. Her body was petite and firm, leaving fantasies lingering in his mind. She was chit-chatting with the woman next to her, probably about the new album from Inconsiderate Roach. He didn't care about what she had to say, only what he had to see.

As she stood, worshipping the band, her clothes started to shrink. Tighter and tighter, it squeezed her body, until they ripped apart and she wore only her supple skin. She screamed and tried to cover herself. Panic swept through her as her hands clasped the back of her head and remained fixed. On display for hundreds of people, she began to cry. Tears streamed down her cheeks and heavy sobs escaped her lips. I hate when they cry! He thought. After a few moments, she was finally able to move. William watched as she escaped into the crowd, seeking shelter from the stares of excited men.

A sneer of madness was displayed on him. The noise was unbearable. It seemed to come from all around him. Many ugly people with piercings yelled and jumped up and down. Mohawks and dreadlocks speckled the overwhelming crowd. Neon lights flicked on and off, posters flapped in the wind trying to break the bondage of cheap adhesive.Yep. These creatures must pay.

Let's start with the noise shall we? William closed his eyes and visualized hundreds of Mimes lounging around a broken carnival. When he opened his eyes, Mr. Mohawk and Mr. Dreadlocks had a look of terror on their painted faces. They formed their mouths around the syllables, but nothing squeaked out.

Somewhere in the Mime Ocean, a cell phone rang out. A very pretty mime, wearing name brand clothing and red stilettos flipped open her phone. "Hello? Hello? Can you hear me?" William laughed maniacally as he watched a mime try to carry on a conversion on a cell. The laughter echoed through the punk mimes, gaining the attention of everyone. Heads slowly turned towards him in confusion. A few of the larger silent enemies came charging towards him. As they pushed through the crowd and stood toe to toe with him, he wiped them out.

Mr. Mohawk was the last to go. He reared back his fist, intending to punish his tormentor, when a large Rottweiler appeared from thin air. The fangs dug deep into his thighs, ripping and shredding. As he silently protested, the vicious dog turned to mist. He retreated backwards, stumbling over his own feet. He landed onto the ground, knocking the wind out of him. Dirt and debris flung high into the air, clouding his view. Horror struck as he watched that same cloud turn into a swarm of red wasps. Stingers first, they dove. When they disappeared the crowd cowered at the image of a dead mime.

William walked through the crowd, uninterrupted to the ticket booth and purchased front row seats. As he sat down among the other occupants, he closed his eyes. They haven't seen anything yet! He thought.

*****

Max watched the worn out conveyor belt carry his luggage through the clunking machinery.

Somewhere, a fat man in a uniform was able to see his unmentionables. How embarrassing, he thought. As he walked through the metal detector, he fought the urge to cheat and disable the alarm. The siren wailed and the red beacon swirled, casting a red glow on the officer's face. He watched as two rent-a-cops came towards him. Armed with the paddles that search his body, Max decided to make it interesting. He focused on the gun strapped to his hip. When they slowly passed the devices across his hip, they found several rolls of quarters.

"Sorry officer, I must have forgotten about them." He slowly handed them the pocket change and submitted himself to one more body sweep. When they were thoroughly satisfied, he took the change and went along his merry way. His gun once again banged against his hip. He walked along the shiny marble floor, losing himself in his own reflection.

He noticed how haggard his face looked. His eyes carried many bags from several nights of sleeplessness. They were yellow. Yellow? Weren't they just green? He felt the sandpaper texture of stubble that threatened a full beard. As he ran his hand across his face, excitement washed over him. A mission. They gave me a mission. After years of persecution, I will finally be free!

He strolled down the aisle of the airplane, carefully maneuvering himself around the tiny carts. No need to disturb the nice servers, is there? He thought to himself. As he shoved his luggage overhead, he grabbed a tiny bottle of Vodka. Settling deeper into his first class seat, he downed the mini drink and relaxed. Sleep overtook his body. A four hour flight and he will be face to face with his destiny.

*****

Inconsiderate Roach! Inconsiderate Roach! What a stupid name. Yet this is what they are cheering. Stupid humans. William watched as four rockers started to play the first song of the night. Screaming and cheering from all around. Horrible auditory pollution assaulted his ears. About the third time into the chorus line William felt hate rising.

" I don't need to share baby...I don't need to share, I got my share, I just take what I want. I don't care if it's fair. I'm just Inconsiderate. Yeah... Inconsiderate." Lasers shot across the dark auditorium, reflecting the cloud of smoke rising from the secret smokers. The grungy singer brought the mic to his lips. This time...another voice came from the amp.

"Attention ugly people. Everyone will die." Protests came from the unbelieving audience. Many threatened refunds, many more simply tried to walk out. Blood came raining down from the ceiling and spikes arose from the floor. Hundreds were impaled. Screams and sobs escaped from the throats of the survivors. William closed his eyes.

Everything went silent. Blood disappeared and the spikes withdrew. Survivors stared at the stage in silent horror. Inconsiderate Roach slowly backed away and tried to run. The heavy thumps of their footsteps clanked noisily as they were stopped in their tracks. One by one, the audience watched as their heads spontaneously exploded. Brain matter and gore sprayed onto the shocked crowd. A fresh sense of impending doom overwhelmed them. William smiled as they trampled their neighbors to death in an attempt to reach the door. Time to end this, he thought.

Spiders. Poisonous spiders came oozing out of every crack in the plaster. Shoelaces from the fallen wiggle and squirm then appear in devilish forms. Fangs drip from the rattle snakes as they coil and strike. Before they knew it, thousands of Black Widows and snake bites finish the job the spikes left behind. As the last pitiful human fell, William gathered the money left on their broken swollen bodies and quietly exited into the night.

*****

The fresh breeze kissed his face when he first hit the streets. Max just wanted to be through with it. But how will I find him? He puzzled over where to begin. Like divine intervention, dozens of sirens blared as the black and white police cruisers whizzed past. These were followed closely by the roar of the ambulances.

Max lights his cigarette and inhaled deeply. The smoke felt wonderful expanding in his lungs. After a long flight, nothing compares to that first cigarette. He reached into his jacket pocket and pulled out a black and white photo. The face of his enemy burned into the back of his mind. He was close; he knew it. One step at a time, he slowly walked towards the chaos.

He heard gunshots ring out in the night. He heard explosions, and screams pierced his eardrums. As he closed in on the scene, he noticed a lone man surrounded by police. They hid behind their cars, doors open and guns drawn. This was it.

He watched for an hour as they battled it out. Max wasn't in any hurry to interfere. He would be the next target if he got involved and incarceration wasn't a part of his plans.

*****

Sergeant Reynolds shook in fear. He was face to face with the devil and was losing. Explosions rang out as the pistols backfired. The police cruisers started to vanish one by one, leaving his officers completely exposed to his madness. Reynolds ducked under his driver side door, releasing a barrage of bullets from his sidearm. He watched in horror as the bullets turned to sand in front of his eyes. The squad beside him had a guillotine drop from above, decapitating them where they stood. The look of terror was still frozen on their faces as their heads rolled between his feet. All was lost and Sergeant Reynolds knew it. A full retreat was ordered.

*****

William gloated internally. The crooked smile overtook his face as he watched the last of the police disappear into the foggy night. He stood unopposed. He walked down the bloodstained stairs and headed into the night. The trees swayed back and forth in the wind, dropping the occasional colored leaf in his path. He was alone. Wasn't he?

He was plagued with paranoia. William picked up his pace as he grew aware. Aware that someone was watching his every move. A large shadow slowly crept into sight. It was small at first, but steadily grew into a large being. Its eyes gleamed in the night sky, burning a bright red. For the first time in his life, William was scared. He watched as the shadow shifted from human to wolf. Then another wolf. A whole pack of shadow wolves howled and snarled.

Max stood proudly behind his pack of wolves intending to finish this. William understood completely. Another lived, but not for long. Fire circled the shadows then consumed them. Fire golems and shadow wolves battled in the night. Meteors fell from the sky, threatening to extinguish the life force from Max. He simply closed his eyes. Tornados sucked up the meteors and flung them forcefully towards their master's head.

After thirty grueling minutes, the war became stagnant with incomprehensible creatures. They were exhausted.

"What do you want?"

"I want you to die. Now die fucker!" Max could feel the hate flow through him

"Bullshit…don't try to stop me or I'll destroy you"

Max took two steps closer to him, making his face visible to his foe. The ground shook and lava flowed from an opening in the asphalt. William could feel the intense heat melt the rubber of his sneakers. The ground suddenly turned soft. The mud absorbed the lava and flowed towards Max. More and more mud pooled together and picked up speed. The mudslide slammed into Max, sweeping him off of his feet. William watched him get sucked to the bottom, sure it was his demise.

To his surprise, the mud turns to dirt. The dirt turns to grass. The grass becomes a forest surrounding him completely. Thorny branches shoot out and grab his arms and legs. The pain was intense and immediate. Completely helpless, William froze, forgetting to concentrate on his enemy. Max slowly walked towards him mumbling something terrible. Loud squawking comes from the thorny branches. Hundreds of yellow eyes appear in the darkness. The birds come by the hundreds ripping at his flesh, chunking it off piece by piece. Max could hear his screams of pain. This was his chance.

He reaches down and feels the cold steel of his gun. Time to finish this! He takes aim, but is too late. The trees disappear, replaced by dozens of homicidal clowns. They charge, with axes held high. His chance was lost. He had to think quickly.

That's it. Quicksand! The ground sinks everything deep to its core. Quickly, he hardens it, turning it to Concrete. Now bound, Max takes aim once more.

The barrel of the gun is reflected in Williams's pupils, fear constricts his airway. Smoke rises and a bright flash of light is the last thing he sees. Max watches his body crumple in place. With a calm demeanor, he returns everything to normal. He reaches into his pocket for his cell, snapping a picture of the carcass for evidence. After lighting a cigarette, he turns and disappears into the quiet of the night.

*****

After another long flight from Seattle, He heads for the shiny office of Dr. Blitz. The windows gleam in the daylight and the gold signing sing praise to his victory. He walks past the receptionist and invades the office. After molding the chair back into his favorite recliner, he slides the cell across the table.

"It is done. Now it is your turn."

Dr. Blitz stares at the picture in amazement. "You work fast."

"That's right. Fast service means fast payment. Now pay up."

For the first time, Max sees a smile on the good doctor's face. "Did you really think it would be that easy?"

"I really did. You turned me from a freak to an assassin. What else do you want, you fuck?"

Dr. Blitz produced another file and slid it across the desk. The photo inside contained not one, but two faces this time. "These are the Morton twins; they have been wreaking havoc in Boise, Idaho."

"Let me guess, Doc, My job isn't done"

"You are a very smart man, bring me pictures of two dead bodies and we will go from there."

"Fine…I will be there first thing in the morning." He felt his temper rise once more as he turned his back on Dr. Blitz.

"Be careful, Max. I would hate to see them beat you this time." A hearty laugh bellowed out of the good Doctor as he watched Max disappear through the doorway.

Intangible: Revelations

Cody Toye

"We are the gods of Chaos and Destruction and you have been judged!" The crowd stood in shocked silence as they gazed upon the faces of the Morton twins. Their long tan monk's robes fluttered in the wind. The tassels of their prayer beads lay upon their stomach, a symbol of their unshaken faith. The cold mountain air ripped through the city of Boise making it difficult to concentrate on anything other than getting warm.

The silence was broken by a single nonbeliever who dared to forsake the new gods. "Who do you think you are? You're lucky we don't climb up those stairs and drag you kicking and screaming to the police station."

The expression on the bald man's face twisted from smirk to agony as his clothes turned into a murder of crows, ripping and tearing at his flesh. When the birds flew, only a former shell of a human remained. Flesh and bone of a tattered corpse lay upon the cold ground, a testament to the raw power of the new found gods.

"Bow…" started Bryan.

"…to us!" Finished Ryan

The crowd dropped to their knees and placed their heads between their hands, tears swelling in their eyes. They intently listened for their next command. Daggers rained upon the ground, making a terrifying sound echo in the silence. No one dared look up from their holy position.

"Faithful servants, prove yourselves in the eyes of your gods."

"We need thirteen of you. Only thirteen."

"Thrust the blade of redemption…"

"…into the flesh of the nonbelievers," finished Bryan.

The crowd scrambled to their feet and dove for the nearest blade, driving it repeatedly into the bodies of their long-time loved ones. Fathers slaughtered sons. Sisters, brothers, and neighbors collided in an epic battle for survival. Some, unable to bear the pain of killing family, gave up and fell where they stood. The blood spilled upon the blacktop, turning the parking lot into a river of blood. When the screams of pain and terror subsided, thirteen blood-soaked followers bowed down to the Morton Twins.

*****

The man in the black trench coat licked the paper and finished rolling his cigarette. He pulled a match from his boot and struck it upon the table. The glow of red and the smell of burning paper repulsed the good doctor.

"I am Doctor Blitz and you are being sentenced for your crimes."

"I don't give a fuck who you are. What do you want?"

The good doctor flipped through the file that lay in front of him. Listing out the many atrocities committed against his country. "Long-shot Trevor McGraw. U.S. Special Forces, sniper. Thirty seven confirmed kills, thirteen solo missions, two medals of Honor and a purple heart. Very impressive! Then you were found freelancing your talents to the Russians and stand accused of treason. You are sentenced to death by firing squad tomorrow morning."

"I know who the hell I am!" Long-shot slammed his fist down and cleared the desk in one massive sweep of his arm.

The good doctor stood staring the man down, trying to hide the fear he was feeling. "I can make it all go away Long-Shot. All you have to do is say yes. One more mission, that's it, and when it's complete you will be a free man. What do you say?"

He crushed the rolled cigarette out on the desk, flipping it at Doctor Blitz. It bounced off of his forehead and landed gracefully in the waste basket next to him. "What is it? What is this mission of yours?"

A photo of Max was slid under his nose, followed by a photo of the Morton twins. "This is Max, he is…um…on a sort of mission himself. He is to destroy them. The doctor tapped the black and white of the twins and waited for a response.

"And…I can't read your fucking mind"

"Max is in over his head this time. They are rapidly gathering followers. He is greatly outnumbered and must complete his task. What I need from you is to silently follow him and pick off everyone else. Do not kill the Morton twins. I need them destroyed by Max."

Long-Shot sighed and stared at the photos once more. "And for this, I will be pardoned?"

"Not quite, you will follow him on all of his missions. When he is completely finished, you will kill Max."

The good doctor watched as Long-Shot walked through his doorway, headed to Idaho. He couldn't decide who scared him more, Max or Long-Shot.

*****

Max knew they would make an appearance. Hundreds flocked to Anne Morrison Park for the Spirit of Boise Balloon Festival. The scenery was amazing. Hot air balloons of every shape and size littered the park. He could see the mountains, smell the fresh air, and truly enjoy the beauty of the outdoors. For once, he was glad to be alive. He was happy to be a part of something so amazing, yet saddened by the thought of the war to come. All of these people, he thought, will be caught in the middle.

He looked upon the crowd, people watching, as his friends once called it. A middle aged man held on to his steaming cup of coffee and was watching the Energizer Bunny prepare for takeoff. He stopped and adjusted his gloves, which had no covering for his fingers.

Strange, Max thought, why would he choose gloves that don't cover his fingers? Isn't it a little cold for that? His focus then turned towards a little girl with pigtails. She was chomping down on some sort of snack and jumping up and down enthusiastically. The pointing and jumping was a sure sign that the sugar had taken effect. Max saw what had stolen her attention away from the balloons.

A clown, walking upon stilts, was creating balloon animals for all of the children. A small parade of inflated wiener dogs floated randomly around the crowd. Something was not quite right about this; it seemed so out of place among the festivities, he thought.

He slowly made his way towards the entertainer, hoping he was wrong. He never took his gaze off of the caked on white and green make-up. He watched in horror as the pleasant smile twisted into a fang filled nightmare. His right eye slowly shifted to an evil red glow and the yellow fingernails grew into sharpened claws. All at once, the balloon animals blinked twice and grew razor-sharp teeth. The gnawing sound was awful. They released themselves from their string prison and randomly attacked onlookers.

Max turned around just in time to watch the Energizer Bunny come alive and smash the middle aged man in one attempt. It rolled through the crowd, leaving no survivors in its path.

"We are the gods of Chaos and Destruction!" The Morton twins ranted "And you have been judged!"

Max ran through the sea of the slaughtered, coming into view of his enemies. The war has begun.

*****

Long-Shot peered over the ledge of the building. Tiny human ants walk around in circles beneath him. As he watched, an incredible urge came over him. With a mighty snort, a large wet drop of spit fell to the ground. The tiny ant in the red dress brought her hand to her head and looked towards the building. He ducked behind the ledge and let out a small giggle. It serves her right, he thought.

The shiny metal briefcase was slowly opened, revealing the contents inside. Between the foam imprints were three parts to a very powerful gun. Long-shot pulled them out and quickly snapped them in place. The large scope slid together with a gentle click and the tripod legs were unfolded. He took his shirt and gently rubbed the glass of the scope, clearing the milky residue from it. He pressed his eye against the glass and swept his view across the crowd. Hundreds walked around, enjoying the sights and doing nothing in particular.

He pulled his eye away and looked at the photo once more. How am I supposed to find one person in a gathering this large? He pulled the pouch of tobacco from his shirt pocket and rolled a cigarette. Blood curdling screams brought him back to the task at hand. He dropped the pouch, spilling the contents all over the rooftop. "Oh Shit!"

He watched as the man's head caved in from the enormous bunny. He swept his view across the crowd to see the evil clown and the balloon monsters. "What the fuck is going on?" He continued his search until he locked his sights on Max. Through the cross-hairs he was able to get a clear view of the man. You are going to stop all of this? He thought to himself.

*****

"Bow…"

"…to us."

The twins stood in the basket of a brightly colored hot air balloon. Thirteen bloody followers surrounded it. The crowd watched as every balloon in the air turned into heavy boulders. A dozen or more people fell from the sky, dying on impact, crushed by the weight of the merciless rocks. Once more they made their announcement. "Bow to us"

Many people dropped to their knees, worshipping the new gods. The ones that stood proud were dealt with swiftly and effectively. The last thing they heard was a high pitched whine as the razors cut through the air and their heads were severed from their bodies.

Max kept his head to the ground, blending in with the crowd. He needed time to analyze the situation. Thus far, he had the element of surprise on his side and planned on using it. As the twins watched the faithful bow, the balloon above them turned into a boulder and came crashing down. Seconds before a painful death, the boulder was turned to a swarm of locusts sent to attack the innocent.

"Who dares to defy their gods?" Terrified, no one said a word. They keep their heads down and prayed for a miracle. "Bring us the women and children. We will show you what happens to the unjust."

One by one, the Morton soldiers left the balloon and walked into the crowd. As the first soldier gripped the arm of an elderly lady, a single gunshot rang out. A small hole in his forehead trickled blood. He fell, shocked and regretful. The remaining soldiers tried to snatch their prey and run, trying to avoid the fate of their brother. Long-Shot plucked them off with considerable ease, leaving only a few.

The twins tried to pinpoint where the attack was coming from but failed. Every building was consumed by fire, an immediate retaliation on their part. Long-Shot felt the heat rising, the flames kissed the metal and moved upwards. Sweat poured from under his hat, his eyes burned and his vision blurred. A few more minutes and he would be toast. Finally, through blurry crosshairs, he was able to take out the remaining soldiers. The rest was up to Max! He ran across the rooftop, desperate to find an escape.

*****

Max rose, standing face to face with them. Their fat bodies and thick glasses made them look less terrifying than they claimed to be.

"You dare…"

"…to challenge the Gods?" they boasted

"The gods? You are not the gods! You are simply self-serving beings waging war on a population that didn't even know you existed. I pity you. Sadly, you must die."

They looked at each other and then back at Max. The intense stare-down lasted for a flat two minutes. Suddenly, a large battery of arrows shot from thin air. Razor sharp points threatened penetration deep in his body. Max closed his eyes. A large boulder rose from the ground, providing shelter from the attack. The arrows snapped and fell to the ground, unable to complete their journey into his innards.

Max smiled. If I can't send them to hell…then I'll bring hell on earth! They watched as a black shadow rose from the ground. It grew bigger and bigger until it was over a hundred feet tall. The eyes shined of fire and the dozens of pointed teeth stayed the size of an average human. Its head split and reformed. Then it split and reformed again. Before them towered Cerberus, the three headed hell hound. The loud low growl and the horrible snarl caused panic in the crowd. It darted snapping and whipping its heads back and forth at the terrible two.

To his surprise, Max watched as they casually dealt with their terrible enemy. From the rocks came a creature crawling on its belly. It slithered and rose. Taller and taller until it was eye level with the beast. Its heads doubled the count of Cerberus, and its breath oozed acid. Max understood completely: Hydra of Lerna, sibling to Cerberus.

They take their religion seriously, he thought. He watched as the creature killed his monster and headed deep into the crowd. Cerberus vanquished into dust and was a mere memory. Thinking back to his studies he strained to remember how to kill them. From the sky, large flaming sickles came spinning towards the Hydra sheering its heads from its body. The intense heat cauterized the cuts, keeping the creature from reproducing its vicious form. It fell, melting away into sand.

Max took advantage of the moment of silence, and brought forth not one, but four Minotaurs. The large creatures wielded battle axes and charged the balloon basket. In blind panic, the twins formed a large metal box around them. The deafening clank against the metal gave way to large dents. A cave-in was apparent. I have them now, he thought as he watched the spectacle. From behind the large creatures came the sound of rattles. Many rattles adorned ugly faces as the Gorgon bodies formed from the crisp mountain atmosphere.

In an instant, the Minotaurs turned and faced the hideous half snake creatures. Their eyes gleamed and their rattles shook. The four bull creatures turned to stone. With a thunderous boom, stone bits exploded into the crowd. He watched as fifteen onlookers were made into human statues.

Thinking fast, he locked the creatures in a large mirrored box. A huge bus fell from the sky shattering the glass and crushing its contents. Each shard of glass raised high into the air and slowly transformed into many twisted versions of the Cyclops. Armed with huge tree trunks, they ravaged everything in their path. As a powerful blow struck the ground, it started to tremble. The basket rose high into the air, propelled upwards by a large mountain. The Morton twins peered down from their new home.

Dark clouds filled the sky, blocking the sun and draining its warmth. Hundreds of lightning bolts struck the monsters immediately turning their bodies into burnt ash. "ENOUGH!"

Everything cleared away. Besides the scarred landscape and the dead bodies, no evidence of the bizarre battle was left. Max knew right away. It was an invitation to take the battle to the sky, to take the fight to the makeshift Mount Olympus. He felt a little uneasy about this, but had no ultimatum.

*****

He watched his briefcase land in the bushes, safely hidden from sight. He once more judged the distance to the billboard. About ten feet, he thought. I know this is going to hurt! He looked behind him and watched the flames creep closer. He could feel the heat trying to enter his body, leaving him no choice but to blindly leap at the billboard. With a running start, he felt his feet leave the sanctuary of the rooftop. He closed his eyes and stretched out his arms. He felt the metal between his fingertips and squeezed them shut with all of his strength. His body slammed into the iron and wood with tremendous force. He was sure he broke a rib or two. When he finally braved the view, he found himself dangling a hundred feet from the ground.

With much effort, he managed to pull himself onto the lip of the sign and slowly make his way to the supporting beams. His feet nimbly moved from one beam to the next, making his way back to the earth below. Finally, with both feet on the ground he hunched over and hurled.

Long-Shot retrieved his weapon from the bush and lay in the grass, wishing he could go to sleep. With a few well trained movements of his hands, the weapon was functional once more. Through the scope he could see two really tall boulders. As the crosshairs followed the rocks, he saw Max and the twins high in the air battling it out.

*****

The war turned drastically. The religious battle turned strange. Birds of every shape and size collided in the air, some real, some fictional. Fire balls and tidal waves extinguished each other. Max could feel his body drain of energy. An hour has passed since this has begun and the Morton twins have not slowed down. The amount of energy it takes to keep this rock in the air is tremendous. How can they keep fighting? He stared at them with a new found respect. With a closer look, the answer came to him in a flash. They are not fighting. Only one is fighting and the other is keeping the mountain underneath them.

He dodged once more as a fireball whizzed past his head. He brought another tidal wave roaring towards them. This time, turning them to bees and attacking only one of them. Bryan opened his eyes in time to see the bees coming, completely losing his focus on the rock. The mountain split into two and chunked of into many smaller boulders. Their bodies went into a free fall towards the ground. Max watched in fascination as they once again avoided a swift death.

They turned the rock slide into a mud slide. As their bodies landed upon the gooey mass, they gracefully slide back to earth. Max started his decent when he felt something cold and slimy wrap around his body. The hissing of the enormous python seemed to climb directly into his head. He struggled against its strength trying to concentrate hard enough to stop its wrath. He had nothing left; he was drained. His eyes closed as he felt consciousness slip away.

*****

Through the crosshairs he watched Max lose. A decision had to be made and it had to be made fast. On one hand, I was told not to kill the Morton twins, he thought to himself. On the other, If Max dies, then my mission is failed and I die. What the Hell…Doctor Bullshit, or whatever his name was, can kiss my ass!

Two well placed shots rang out into the day, bringing the vicious battle to an end. Both Bryan and Ryan Morton's bodies bounced off of the cold ground with a horrid thud. He slowly packed up his weapon and lit his cigarette. Among the screaming and running citizens of Boise, Idaho, Long-Shot McGraw casually disappeared without a trace.

*****

Max awoke amazed he was still alive. He remembered the snake, the nasty creature would make appearances in his dreams, and this much he was sure of. He struggled to remember what happened. He could see their ugly faces laughing at him and could vaguely remember a couple of small bangs rippling in his eardrums. Then…the snake was gone.

He shook his head once more and ordered another couple of tiny vodkas from the flight attendant. As he tossed the small lid aside and downed the first bottle, a vivid realization came crashing down on him. He had help. Someone killed them for me and let me take the credit. Max was shocked.

He brought his bruised and battered arm towards his pocket and thrust his hand deep inside. As he silently turned on his cell phone, he stared at the pictures with morbid fascination. The bodies of the Morton twins lay side by side with tiny bullet holes inside their mouths. A perfect shot that was hidden by the position of the bodies. If he didn't know what to look for he would have missed it completely. The question isn't who, he thought, but rather whose side is this person playing for?

*****

The good doctor slid another folder in front of Max and smiled. "I'm glad to see you won the day!"

"I didn't. Someone else did."

"Oh, how's that? You are standing and they are not. I would call that a victory wouldn't you?"

"Cut the shit Doc. We both know I had help on this one."

Doctor Blitz stared at Max trying to keep his anger in check. "I don't know what you are talking about Max. Are you saying that you didn't kill them?"

"That's right Doc. I didn't kill them."

"Then who did? Hundreds of witnesses say you slayed the Morton twins. Are they lying Max?"

"Yep." Max opened the folder and stared at the photo inside. A wave of relief washed over him. He searched the contents twice but still found only one photo this time.

"That is Orlando Scranton, native to Texas. By trade he is a meteorologist. However, his predictions only come true because he causes them to. Might want bring an umbrella with you this time Max. It's hurricane season." He could hear the Good Doctor laugh at him as he slowly limped out of the front door and made his way into the daylight.

*****

"Didn't I tell you not to kill them? Didn't I tell you? GODDAMNIT I TOLD YOU NOT TO KILL THEM!"

Long-shot stepped out of the shadows in the corner and sat down at the desk. His face was bold and his eyes steely. "You told me Max had to win. He lost. I had to finish the job."

"You know he is on to you now. He knows. If he spots you, he WILL kill you."

"Let me worry about that"

"That's not the point. We have rules."

"You knew I liked to break the rules when you got me involved. Now deal with the hand you were dealt."

He tipped his hat to the good Doctor and disappeared. This time headed to Texas.

Dribbles the Squirrel Series

Note to Readers:

Everyone has had a job they despised. A job so bad, that you would seriously consider bringing the company to its knees if ever given the opportunity. Now take that rage and funnel it into something useful. That was the purpose of this lovable squirrel, to help me exact revenge on my company. Even if this was only a brutal glimpse into the mind of an overworked and underpaid writer, it sure relieved a lot of anguish along the way. After finishing the series, I watched in awe as its numbers climbed the charts. A small following of the overworked continued to revel in my madness for a bit. I hope you do too. Here is the entire series from beginning to end. Enjoy!

Operation Coffee Deprivation

Cody Toye

"After watching your performance this quarter and keeping a close eye on our profit margin, we have decided to let you go. You have served our blah to the fullest blah and blah blah." Bob watched the bald spot pulse as Mr. Jefferson attempted to explain why he was firing him after twenty five years. In the business world, Bob was a little slow. He focused primarily on computer programming and didn't care about profit margins.

A small chuckle hiccupped out of his throat as he remembered the picture he had encrypted into the last email of his career. The bald head of Mr. Jefferson appeared with a nice black line through it. The line, perfectly drawn over the rough bald noggin portrayed his true feelings for the man. Every time the email gets forwarded, the recipient would be in for a surprise. Bob was certain the butt crack joke would be seen by all the big spenders before it was said and done. This thought alone was better than anything they could offer him for his time.

Anger crept into his blood stream, turning his complexion a strawberry tint. The more words that spewed from the mouth of the traitor, the harder it became to concentrate. The blah blahs were replaced with a fictitious underlying meaning.

"So... in short Bob, I am a jerk! I'm ugly and bald and make three times your salary. I will get a huge bonus if I fire you. I will then pay someone six dollars and hour less to do your job. I know it was you pooping in the plant holders in the lobby, (it was) so security will show you out. Oh, by the way Bob, My brand new red Porsche is not scratch proof, so feel free to use your sharpest car keys to teach me a lesson!"

A large sigh squeezed its way out of his lungs. This, followed by the slow movement of his defeated body rising from the cold wooden chair was the only response he could manage. He knew Mr. Jefferson didn't say anything remotely close to that but didn't care. One black loafer in front of the other he walked. He walked slowly to the door feeling the dead glare of an over-rated man burrow into the back of his skull.

Two sharply dressed security officers waited for him on the other side of the door. Slowly, the curvy golden handle of the office door turned. Slam. Slam. After the third hard smash, Bob managed to get escorted down the long corridor towards the lobby. The checkered marble seemed to taunt him as shame grew deep within. The colors seemed even more vivid than he remembered.

Stomping past the water fountain, he spotted three corporate slackers telling the same jokes as always. He slowly turned towards them with a crooked smile upon his face. By now, he was sure that word had swept through the office at sub-atomic speeds. Not only that, but it managed to make it to Jupiter and back. Right now some poor schmuck of an alien is pointing his finger down to Earth and laughing at him. They all knew, he was sure of it.

Silence fell upon the room. They were waiting on him to leave. Waiting on him to hold his head down in shame and march out of the office. He was going to have none of it... no way... not a chance. Bob did the opposite. Standing upon the shadows of three very important men, something very unexpected happened. He laughed. He not only laughed but gasped for air. Tears streamed down his cheeks and his foot thumped against the floor echoing through the entire room.

About the time he started dipping his tie into the water fountain and sucking the water off, those same nicely dressed security guards walked him out of his office for good. The Last thing anyone remembers Bob saying that day was "Beware of the squirrels in diapers, they don't understand Greek." Bob slowly walked towards the yellow curb. Random thoughts plagued him as he sat down and wept. "Twenty five years of my life gone." He thought glumly of the memories from his years of servitude and found it ironic how much time was spent wishing for a different job.

*****

Life went on at Q.J. Enterprises and after awhile everyone forgot about poor Bob. They went about their day like any good zombie would. As for Bob, he remembered every single one of them. He became consumed with hatred so deep that he spent every penny he had on revenge. He wasn't crazy that day, oh no, he knew exactly what he was saying. He wasn't crazy at all, just very well organized. His whole retirement fund was spent at a local pet store. Two hundred squirrels had found a new home that day; all of them recruited into Bob's army.

It took two months to do it, but Bob finished his computer program. He used images of acorns, walnuts, and others to brain-wash his miniature minions. Squirrel after squirrel ran his elaborate obstacle course, learning how to do specific tasks. Then there was the best of the best, the Green Beret of the squirrel world. This squad, led by Dribbles the squirrel, learned a multitude of tasks that needed to be carried out. One by one he worked with them all until they were ready to take on the world. He started small, experimenting on local citizens. His mission was simple: minor annoyance.

*****

The sun was shining brightly that morning when Bob loaded his mini-van of doom. A warm fuzzy feeling exploded deep within his stomach. For the first time in a very long time, Bob was in a great mood! The mini-van swept across the bi-pass at tremendous speeds. He turned the music up full blast, forcing the sound to penetrate his glass windows and keep the outside world company. His head slowly bobbed to the music while weaving in and out of traffic. Mrs. Smith did not know how to react to what just happened.

She was in the middle of her morning commute, doing her usual talk on the cell phone and drive routine. All of a sudden, a mini-van with speeds exceeding seventy miles per hour weaved in front of her. This would have been normal, except the middle aged man behind the wheel was head banging to Mozart. She watched as the maniac did the same thing to the next two cars in line. His excess speeds then slowed to a crawl as he very carefully made a left into the Public Library. All she could do was shake her head. "It must have been something he ate," she thought. The small red mini-van pulled into an isolated spot and parked.

*****

Students came in and out, never once bothering to give him the time of day. The cool wind and warm spring sun drew a large crowd into the outside world. "A perfect day for a test run," he thought to himself. Bob opened the door to his van and stretched his legs. He felt the excitement build as he opened the back door and released the lock on the cage. The clink of freedom sent Dribbles flying out of his cage in a panic. He jumped, he scurried, he flicked his cute bushy tail then disappeared behind a large shrub.

Jimmy had just finished his homework and was shuffling his books back and forth, jockeying for a good grip. A balancing act that was almost impossible to perform. Papers tried their best to fly away, but to no avail. Four hours in a library simply meant that Jimmy was more determined to keep the papers than the wind was to take them from him. "One more Saturday gone forever!" he thought to himself. A sigh of relief and a sense of accomplishment overwhelmed his senses. He thought he might never get to see another weekend as a free man, but this is the last assignment he has to turn in. "This is it," he thought as he slowly made it down the sidewalk towards his freedom "I am done"

At first Jimmy had no idea what had happened. A furry brown blur streaked across his line of sight momentarily confusing him. Books flew to the ground, papers scattered in the wind, and Jimmy stood there shocked, mouth open and eyes bugged. "Wow, that squirrel is a Jerk" he thought to himself. A quick flick and a brief jump, Dribbles lay his head down inside the cage.

*****

"It worked, my program actually worked!" the sinister smile felt comfortable on his face as visions of what lay ahead appeared in a thick fog before him. Clink. Clink. Bob locked the cage and headed home. The drive seemed to never end and impatience swelled deep inside. "One hour to prepare, one hour to exact my revenge!" The sweat retreated from his forehead as he led every single squirrel into their steal prison cells. Two hundred cages turned his living room into a perpetual petting zoo. The lack of space in his vehicle meant he would have to take one mission at a time. Bob rattled happy thoughts around his cranium, realizing it would be better this way. "I can make them suffer, over and over again!" He understood how sadistic it was to torture them over a long period of time but didn't care.

"No less than they deserve. Did they care that I missed out on a raise three years in a row?

Did they care when they fired me without even blinking?" Bob recalled every little detail of their treachery and was replaying it over and over in his mind. Cartoons flowed through his mind like water through a faucet. A strange, yet satisfying version of Spy vs. Spy twisted his thoughts. In this version though, the black spy was a squirrel, and the white spy stays huddled in the corner crying for his mommy.

*****

The morning sun just peaked over the horizon when Art pulled into his usual parking spot. A sanctuary he began to call his home over the years. One more "hair check" and he was off to start the day. The smell of the dew on the grass and the glimmer of the golden sign above the revolving door reminded him of how great it was to be him. As he pushed into the lobby a whole heard of "Good morning Mr. Conway" resonated in his ear canals. With a smile upon his face he headed towards his private office.

He no more than relaxed his body in his Italian Leather chair when the door creaked open. The sound of the un-oiled hinges grated on his nerves. "This early in the morning no one should have to hear that!" He thought to himself.

"Here's your cup of coffee Mr. Conway."

Art slowly took the coffee from his secretary and placed it upon his desk. The steam started fogging up his glasses in an instant. "Thank you Janelle." He said through a smile.

"You're very welcome Sir. If there is anything else I can help with don't hesitate to ask." Janelle forced a smile back but was having trouble coping with her personal assistant position. "Four years of college and I become a secretary? How fair is that?" She muttered under her breath. Her foot no more than graced the presence of the doorway when his voice called to her.

"There is something you can help me with. I have several meetings and a deadline to meet today; if you can oil my door I would appreciate it."

"No problem Sir" she muttered. What, now I am the maintenance man too? If I could just tell him off…but bills have to get paid. She started to angrily stomp out the door when she was interrupted once again.

"Oh, and Janelle…"

She turned to face him, trying to keep very calm. Inhale and exhale wwwooosh. "Yes Sir"

"If you could keep the coffee coming it would make my day. Long hours ahead of me you know" Art smiled once again, but this time she could tell it was a simple power play, a gesture to show that he is in control and she is nothing more than a servant.

"No problem sir!" Came the short reply. With that, she snuck quietly out into the lobby.

Art drank his coffee and worked on his memos all day long. The sun beat high in the sky, casting a light shadow through his window. The clock ticked with all its might and tocked as well. Finally, noon rolled around. To Art, this meant lunchtime was upon him. He knew this not because the clock struck high noon, but because he said so. He didn't need the clock to tell him it was lunch-time, he was in control, he told the clock it was lunch-time. His stomach just dictated when he would do so. Today, his stomach says lunchtime is at noon. He marched through the office enjoying his normal chit-chat with the worker bees and had his fifteen minutes of cooler talk before heading to the lobby.

The lobby, in its own fanciful way, was a replica of how he felt inside himself today. The warm glow of the gold inlays and the marble counter tops showed elegance and power. After all, who's more elegant and powerful than a Chief Executive Officer of Q.J. Enterprises? He thought to himself.

Looking around the room, he noticed how happy everyone seemed to be at that moment. What Art couldn't understand is the why. Why were they okay sharing lunchtime fables with other worker bees? Why are they happy with the horrible paychecks we give them? Finally, why don't they ever talk to me? This was the ultimate why and to Art, this was a hard one. "I make more money than them, I have my own office, I am an interesting man. Why do they never invite me to sit down and share lunchtime fables?" For a moment, sadness tried to hitch a ride on the emotion train. This was very brief though, as it only took a moment longer for him to realize who he was.

An hour later and a stomach fuller, he made his way back to his office. Meetings came and went but his work seemed to pile up on him. His eyes, now fully packed for vacation, started to show bags. He drank his coffee all day but it didn't seem to help.

He slowly dragged his heavy finger to the intercom and pushed the large button. He knew this was the right button because he forced his secretary to test it three times this week. Just like last week, the button has not moved. "Janelle. Janelle, can you come in here please?" Thick static is the only reply he got. Wait…noise came from the magic box after all. On the other end was a deep voice with a Hispanic accent.

"Janelle went home sick today Mr. Conway." Krrrhh. "Is there anything I can do?"

"Never mind I'll do it myself." He released the button and rushed through the door. Bam. The sound of wood on wood startled everyone within a ten cubicle radius. Phone calls were put on hold, sentences left unuttered. Everyone stopped what they were doing to watch this spectacle. "They don't pay me enough" he grumbled "Imagine, me, Mr. Conway, making my own coffee. Someone should get fired that's what I say. Grumble, grumble, grumble.

Everyone knew if they snickered they were canned. Everyone in the vicinity bit their lower lips as the great Mr. Conway... smarter than they would ever hope to be... fought bravely with the coffeepot and lost. Water overflowed, filters fell from the cabinet making a huge mess all over the floor. After about ten minutes he managed to get it right and reached up into the cabinet to pull down the coffee. That was the moment of his undoing.

Four cabinets and a drawer opened simultaneously dropping supplies all over the place. Every container of coffee fell to the floor exploding into a mini bean mushroom cloud. Sugar fell from sky; coffee- filters and stir-sticks danced briefly in the air before settling down for the night. The whole area looked like the aftermath of a natural disaster on a destructive rampage.

Then, five pesky squirrels in diapers bounced off of the cabinet and disappeared into the quiet office. Art just stood there. The initial shock left him confused and angry. He marched through the ten cubicles and into his office. He sat quietly for a brief moment, trying to calm the rising anger. The more he tried, the worse it got. The wildlife wants to play games, let's play! He thought. First, he pulled up the order sheet and ordered more office supplies; then he hired an exterminator. "I'll give you a reason to wear those diapers!" He mumbled faster and faster until his order was ready to get placed.

His fat finger came crashing down onto something cold. "Cold? Is that right?" When he glanced down he noticed his 'Enter' key was missing. To the logical mind, this is nothing more than an inconvenience. After all, you can still hit 'Enter' without the key can't you? That's not quite how it works though. Art is far too important to use logic. That is why he pays his workers! The world would have to end before he used an incomplete keyboard.

He threw his pencil holder across the room making an even bigger mess. Now, in the office next to him, he got ready to boot up the computer. No 'Enter' key. "You have got to be kidding me," he thought as he stomped back into the cubicle area. "Nope, nope, nope, and nope." Not a single keyboard had the almighty 'Enter'. In a panic, He rushed back to his office, about killing the fern that adorned the waiting room. His finger, now shaking, pressed the big button once more. "Mr. Jefferson. Mr. Jefferson? Mr. Jefferson, pick up. This is Art. This is an emergency! Mr. Jefferson, pick up." No answer.

Operation Blackout

Cody Toye

Dribbles clung tightly to the wildly swinging intercom wires like Tarzan's pet rodent. Mr. Jefferson was none the wiser. Only one floor below him, the entire accounting department was in chaos. Bob loved it. The scene unfolded through two tiny binocular lenses, his beloved Dribbles was poised for phase two.

The sun beat down on him; leaving sweat stains on his new shirt. Bob did not care. This was worth it. To him, watching his plan work perfectly may have its costs, but it was worth every bead of sweat his body could produce. The Mini-van stayed parked on the far edge the parking lot which was reserved for the lower class new hires. No one ever pays attention to the inhabitants here.

Bob opens his door letting the fresh air invade the confined space. What a wonderful day it turned out to be. The birds chirped a happy chirp, the sun smiled and the shrubs stood proud, showing off their new manicures. His legs screamed at him as they tried to support the weight of the rest of his body. Several hours in the cramped cab takes its toll.

He trudged, one step at a time, towards the back hatch. When he was certain no one was watching he lifted it with a mighty pull. The chattering of the twenty squirrels was music to his ears. They twitched their little noses and flicked their bushy tails. A sign they were ready to obey.

Bob felt the heat radiate off of the metal wires of the cages. Silence fell upon the mini-van. Forty blank beady eyes stared at their master, hoping and waiting for their freedom. "That's right, I am your Master. Obey me tiny minions and destroy all I oppose. Mwahaha." His words echoed back into his ears, scaring poor Bob.

His thumb and first finger wrapped around the latches releasing chaos, one by one, into Q.J. Enterprise. The second wave has begun. The squirrels scurried across the blacktop, zigzagging back and forth. Some jumped over the shrubs, others ran through it. Nothing would distract them from their goals.

What a sight to see, Bob couldn't stop smiling as he watched twenty overfed squirrels try to wedge themselves into the rain gutter. He hoped everything would go as planned, but as life taught him, it rarely did.

Panic set in as he watched fifteen squirrels make it inside the gutter. The sixteenth one was not so lucky. It pushed. It scratched. It got its fat furry butt wedged in the opening. The squirrel flailed its tail back and forth and produced a screeching sound that reminded him of a cross between fingernails on a blackboard and an off-balanced washing machine. This sound was sure to draw attention.

The stress built-up and squeezed Bob's heart muscle. His chest lifted and lowered. Bob watched anxiously, hoping the other four squirrels would be smart enough to gain access through an alternate route. No luck! The other four squirrels piled upon each other trying to climb into the rain gutter. Each attempt forced a louder shriek to ricochet through the gutter. After having exhausted all their energy, four fat furry squirrels gave up.

Bob watched as they curled up and went to sleep right where they stood and where they could easily be spotted. "You got to be kidding me!" Bob slumped down in his chair hoping to become invisible. Things couldn't get worse.

*****

Mr. Jefferson swiveled his chair to face the flat screen monitor. He nimbly adjusted his tie and straightened his marble and gold name plate. His meeting with Mr. Matsumoto is about to begin and he only has one chance for a great impression. This account is worth millions and he can't afford to blow it.

Once more, he checked his files. The email detailing his marketing budget and labor costs was sent at exactly 2:05 pm. Files, check. Name plate, check. Best suit and tie in my wardrobe, check. "What could I be missing? Think. Think." He turned his chair around in a smooth arc and micro-adjusted the family portrait that stood on the shelf behind him. After making sure it would be visible during the video-conference, Mr. Jefferson assumed the position in front of the monitor.

Mr. Matsumoto is a family man. Family values are very important to us at Q.J. Enterprise. Important enough to fake for a short duration while the business man forks over enough money to carry by the shovel-full. "Here we go." Mr. Jefferson inhaled deeply one last time before turning the monitor on. With a fake smile on his face, he waited patiently for the conference to begin.

"Mr. Matsumoto, how wonderful it is to finally meet you!"

"The honor is all mine, Mr. Jefferson."

The Japanese business man sighs in disgust as he notices the family portrait adorning the shelf behind him. Americans always put on cheap, fleeting values to impress him. He knew from the reports that Mr. Jefferson was recently divorced. An act such as this says something to him, it says that Mr. Jefferson must think he is dumb enough to invest without researching any weakness in the company. Shame on him. Let's get this over with, he thought to himself.

"I have been looking over your quarterly reports, Mr. Jefferson, and I must say, pretty impressive work. I do however, wonder how much of my money will be spent on advertising and wages."

The moment was at hand, He could not help but to gloat internally. Mr. Jefferson took great strides to lower labor costs and abuse statistics in his favor. This email meant a big promotion; he could feel it in his bones.

"I have sent an email detailing how much of your hard earned money will be spent. Better than that, Mr. Matsumoto, I have outlined how much more money will come flooding into your bank account. Check your inbox."

The silence was unbearable as the screen turned blue. Mr. Matsumoto checked out momentarily while he searched his emails. Mr. Jefferson did a little happy dance and crossed his fingers. I have him by the wallet now, he smugly thought. Click. The screen turned back on. Excitement built inside Mr. Jefferson, knowing good things were ahead. The reply baffled him.

Laughing… large bursts of laughter. This is the reply he got from the Japanese investor. On the screen he saw one skinny finger point at the computer and snorting a laugh. Mr. Jefferson worked so hard to manipulate these statistics, this is not acceptable.

"Do you see the potential our company has Mr. Matsumoto? I can personally build the bridge to financial security for the both of us". No reply came from the investor. Instead, more laughter came rumbling over the screen. "I know we are new at this Mr. Matsumoto, but it is not our custom to laugh at potential partners. Would you like to share what is so funny?"

Taking large gasps of breath and wiping the corner of his eyes with a monogrammed silk handkerchief, the reply came flooding out, "You are a butt-head."

"I beg your pardon? Did I hear you right?"

The face of the American Finance Director became as bright as a rose in springtime. His face scrunched and his teeth clenched.

"You are a butt-head, Mr. Jefferson."

"If you don't want to invest, Mr. Matsumoto, then just say so. I will not tolerate being insulted."

"The email you sent me has nothing but a picture of your head made out to look like a butt. Call us back when you become a professional."

Click. The last thing he heard was giggles from the world's largest industrial investor. He could almost hear the money being flushed down a large toilet. How sad. He didn't think his day could get any worse. He spun around in his chair and flung the family portrait across the room shattering the glass and making a huge mess.

His precious finger came crashing down on the intercom button. He had never needed a drink as badly as he needed right now. "Lindsey, could you bring me a scotch? Lindsey?" No reply. "What is wrong with this blasted thing? Just great." He knelt down in his five hundred dollar suit to look for a solution.

He could go get his own drink, but decided to fix the intercom instead. His hand traced the back of the intercom feeling the cool edges. He felt an empty hole where the cord calls home. As he examined his office further, he found the cord sleeping on the job. If it was an employee, it would be on the unemployment train by now. With a gentle click, the two ends were forced to meet. "There, that should do it. At least something is going right." He mumbled. He smashed the button once more; sure his Scotch would be in his hands momentarily.

"Lindsey, could you bring me a …" Complete darkness surrounded him. A black-out at high noon.

*****

Dribbles clung to the plastic switch controlling the second floor, a balancing act between the ground and the breaker box. Bob watched from the van, as the entire quadrant darkened. "Certainly this will still work. I mean, we are only short five squirrels. Stupid squirrels." He watched as the maintenance man came stomping out the front doors on a mission.

*****

He was to fix the electricity or else. So says Mr. Jefferson. He inhaled the fresh air, breathing deeply, trying to purge the lack of self-respect.

"Fifteen years with the company and they don't even know my name," he grumbled to himself. His hand instinctively slid over the patch embroidered onto his coveralls. Conway. That's funny. I spent the last thirty five years as Craig.

Apparently my name changed to Conway when I sold my soul to this company.

Fix the electric Conway, Fix the plumbing Conway, punch me in the face and call me an asshole Craig! Um…Conway. My application was for the Accounting department. I hold a Bachelor's degree in Business Management and an Associate's degree in Accounting. Many qualifications for a top position here, but the biggest qualification of all is my handle-bar mustache. It states that I know how to fix things big and small without hesitation. I can barely change a light bulb, let along fix the electric.

A job is a job. A large depressing sigh came barreling out, forcing his muscles to loosen and his body to slump. His hand released the tool from his tool belt. His friends call this a Crescent Wrench; he calls it the chompy thingy mcbob that keeps banging into his hip.

He took one big step over the sleeping squirrels trying not to disturb them. He knew they were there, but didn't care. It wasn't his job to remove pests. Besides, he thought to himself, maybe they will attack Mr. Jefferson. That would be awesome. He could picture five squirrels completely destroying his office and breaking the pictures adorning the shelves behind him.

The gnawing and gnawing of wood and metal would be music to my ears. They would chew up all the superficial accomplishments the man had bestowed upon himself. He would swat, he would swear, and he would scream for Lindsey to save him. When he was at his breaking point, I would rush in there and say "Mr. Jefferson, I wish I could help you, but you told me this morning not to do anything that was not in my job description. You don't pay me to think. Just repair the electric. Yep, the electric is fine in here, have a good day!" I think I will leave them sleeping.

Bob watched in amazement as the maintenance man stepped over the squirrels as if it was an everyday occurrence. Things somehow managed to work themselves out. Bob smiled. Conway slowly walked around the corner of the office building, avoiding the shrubs that hug the sidewalk.

When he got to the breaker box, a tiny squirrel in a diaper scurried up the massive Oak tree. He didn't even pause. Why not? he thought to himself. He flipped the breaker and with a loud click, power was restored to the second floor.

*****

When the lights came back on, a loud cheer rose from the workers. This lasted exactly thirty seconds. Nothing but the computer and printer remained on their desks. The staplers, the paperclips, the white-out, and even the tiny pushpins that lay in waiting on the corkboards mounted on the cubicle walls behind them were gone.

The worker bees where in an uproar! Screams and threats came like a barrage of cannonballs towards the workers next to them. Something had to be done. Mr. Jefferson knew exactly what to do. "Lindsey... Lindsey, could you come in here please? Lindsey?" His finger pressed the button harder and harder but no reply came.

He lifted the intercom off of his desk, watching the cord sway back and forth. The copper wires gleamed in the florescent light; tiny plastic bits were sheared off in small chunks. It had been gnawed through. For the second time today, Mr. Jefferson could feel his blood pressure shoot to dangerous levels.

His hands straightened the toupee that attempted to cover his bald head, making him feel just a little better about himself. With a grunt and a little effort, he rose from his Italian Leather rump rest. He no more than straightened his body when darkness suffocated his surroundings. He dexterously found his way to the double paned window. With a little effort, he heaved it open and yelled at the top of his lungs "CONWAY! FIX THE ELECTRIC!"

*****

He just exited the elevator on the second floor when he heard it. Little scratchy noises. Little scratchy noises followed by the devil bidding for his attention. Everything was dark once again. His handle-bar mustache twitched and stretched as he attempted a smile. I love those squirrels! He thought to himself. His footsteps were slow and steady, as he navigated the dark office. After about five minutes of touch and go, he made it to the sunlight.

His eyes struggled to accommodate the invasion of light in pupils, making his job just that much harder. He calmly walked back to the breaker-box and flipped the little switch. Immediately the lights came back on... Conway sat down on the curb and lit a cigarette. The smoke swirled deep into his lungs. He was in no hurry. Conway knew the lights would go out once again. Right on cue, the little squirrel came running down the Oak tree and straight towards him. This is awesome! He thought.

*****

Mr. Jefferson was relieved when the darkness was vanquished. The fear was paralyzing.

As the only big-wig that is afraid of the dark, he thought, I must maintain my composure. He once again stood and attempted to straighten his hair piece. A damp and sticky residue ran down his bald head.

Something was different. A black blob slowly scurried across the gleaming floor. It made it under the door and out into the general population. BANG. The door flew open and a very angry Mr. Jefferson scurried behind it. Laughter erupted. Fingers were pointed. Every worker suddenly forgot why they were mad to begin with. It zigged, it zagged, it ran underneath cubicles. Mr. Jefferson was just a bit faster.

He huffed, he grunted, and he dove seconds before his toupee made it out into the lobby. He had it now. He hung onto it with all his might and felt it struggle beneath his grip. Loud chirpy squeaky sounds rang out, but he did not care. Nobodies hair, not even his own, will make a mockery of the great Mr. Jefferson.

Little clicks and flashes came as employees took pictures from their cell phones. Tomorrow, he would be a YouTube star! Darkness forced his grip loose. He could hear the daring hair escape from him.

*****

"CONWAY!" The little man watched the squirrel once again scurry up the mighty Oak. Click. He flipped the switch once more. As he sat down, he wondered if he had ever had an easier job.

*****

It happened so fast that it blew his mind. One moment he was struggling with his toupee, the next it was dangling from the ceiling fan ten feet in the air. In the span of only a few seconds, every keyboard had been stripped down to its bare essentials. The cords all have been chewed through on the phones and intercom system.

Not a single trace of any office supply remained. One thing became very clear, Q.J. Enterprise was under attack. With one big piqued step, Mr. Jefferson headed through the lobby and towards the elevator. Loud bursts of angry complaints threatened to tear down the very fabric of existence of the mighty empire.

He was sure if he didn't get to the bottom of this soon; he would have many workers leave, never to return. The stares of uncertainty burned into him as he passed by. Blame was a powerful weapon. A weapon when wielded correctly can turn the most successful man into a pile of mush in just mere moments. He felt the sting. He felt the blame cut deep. With each step, hushed whispers and indignant laughs brought him to his boiling point.

He just passed the fern near the waiting area and made it into the elevator when he first heard the chattering. As the metal doors started to squeeze shut, he caught a glimpse of many brown furry bodies scamper into view. Now isolated from the insanity, Mr. Jefferson started to relax. Isolation never felt so good, he thought to himself. On the next floor sits Mr. Quinten, Co-owner of Q.J. Enterprise. If anyone knows what to do, it would be him.

He felt the large metal box start the ascent towards his fearless leader. The clunky device moved in the most awkward manner possible. It rumbled, it shook, and it finally made it to its destination. Mr. Jefferson felt the sudden drop from underneath as the elevator connected with the third floor. He heard the ding, but the doors never opened. Instead, another blackout prevented his escape.

He edged toward the rear until his back connected with the handrail. His body slowly slid down the wall. He sat with his legs curled in his arms and began to rock back and forth. Thick tears streamed down his face, a small trickle at first, then the floodgate opened near his eye sockets. His worst fear had happened. Claustrophobia set in.

Visions of the elevator cable snapping and him falling to his demise twisted his imagination and clouded his judgment. He screamed. He pounded his fists on the metal and screamed at the top of his lungs. His throat became scratchy and raw as he repeated a single name over and over. Lindsey. No one heard his cries for help. Almost no one.

Three floors below sat a maintenance man smiling as the word Lindsey escaped from a vent in the building and echoed into the parking lot. Just when Mr. Jefferson thought he couldn't take anymore punishment, he heard the chattering once more. The chattering became louder and louder, until it was replaced with scratching noises. They were in here with him, he was sure of it.

*****

He felt something soft and fuzzy brush the side of his neck, then the side of his leg. They were everywhere! They were everywhere and nowhere all at once. Only his imagination could tell him what they looked like and how many there were. They had red glowing eyes and razor sharp teeth. They stood at least four foot of pure muscle and breathed fire. There had to be at least four thousand of them. This was for certain.

He swatted randomly at the invisible foes, thrashing here and there, but not a single squirrel fell in battle. His screams went from panic to blood-curdling in a single note. Now he was heard. Loud footsteps came charging towards the elevator on the third floor. Mr. Quinten and Mr. Johnson found their way towards the coward moments before the power came back on.

As his eyes adjusted to the light, Mr. Jefferson at last saw his rivals. Two overly cuddly squirrels lay fast asleep in the corner. He walked over towards them and kicked as hard as he could. The large black loafer came into contact with the metal, radiating pain from his foot into his hip. Cuss words came, anger rose, and his arms swung wildly. The squirrels, now agitated, attacked head on, ripping and shredding the expensive suit into many pieces. Focused on the pain and humiliation, he never noticed them disappear.

*****

Their jaws dropped. They couldn't believe what was inside the elevator. Was he overworked? Inside the elevator was a tattered, bald, Mr. Jefferson cussing and flailing wildly at nothing in particular. "Mr. Jefferson!" He turned and slowly faced his Masters. "May I ask what you are doing in there?"

He spoke through a twisted smile. "I'm bashing them good, Sir." That is all it took, he was fired on the spot. An anonymous call was made to Keeling Institute regarding Mr. Jefferson's mental state. As the two executives made it back down the hallway, oblivious of the chaos beneath, a furry brown tail flicked silently inside of Mr. Quinten's briefcase.

Operation Blackmail

Cody Toye

"I know! I'm looking at the invoice sitting in front of me and I don't remember signing off on it. What do mean it has already been scheduled? This is my company and nothing goes on without my say so…Do you understand me? Who called it in? Art? Art Reddings? He is no longer with the co… Fifty dollars if I cancel? Fine! Send the Exterminator. Tomorrow afternoon. Fine, fine, I got it!"

Mr. Quinten slammed the phone down with tremendous anger, causing the receiver to bounce off of the base. After a quick adjustment, He melted deep in his chair. The Company was losing more and more money and he could feel the pinch in his back pocket. His Mahogany desk lay littered with paperwork, mostly invoices for outlandish office supplies he had to sign off on. Names. Names of the unlucky souls who made the black list of termination floated through his mind. If they cost me money, they do me no good he thought to himself.

He slowly reaches below his desk and carefully pulls the bottle of scotch from the mini-fridge, shaking his wrist to ensure his Rolex would remain scratch free. The cheery clank of the frosted glass against the desk seemed soothing. The strong burn in his stomach from the drink did little to calm his demeanor. He stared at the faux golf course overlapping his work space and decided a small break would do him some good. He pushed the paperwork to the side, almost knocking off the memo from the workers, addressed to him with the utmost concern.

His hairy wrist remained straight as he diligently swung the club. The tiny golf ball carved a perfect path towards the hole, keeping its title as the most reliable thing in his corporation. He would marvel on how it would always do exactly what he wanted and never have to be told twice. As the ball dropped into a hole in one, the satisfying click finally helped him relax enough to focus on the task at hand.

He poured himself one more drink before settling in front of the mountain of paperwork. Certain that a full day's labor was in his future, he pulled the sheet from the top of the stack and stared at it in shock. In his many years as a business man, he had never encountered anything quite like this and it frightened him.

*****

The dark sunglasses were hard to see out of. The long black wig was hot and the uniform was a little too tight. Bob stared at his reflection in the mirror with morbid fascination. My disguise as a delivery man may get me through those doors yet he thought. He readjusted the rearview in his mini-van and climbed out of driver's seat. He slowly treaded the blacktop he used to call home and headed through the gleaming doors of Q.J. Enterprises. The shrub in the lobby brought fond memories flooding back as he brought the package to the receptionist on duty. Duty…Bob snickers. He remembers the shrub in that sense as well. He recalled leaving a small brown package there too! Bob burst out laughing, bringing unneeded attention to himself. Thinking fast, he rambled an explanation to receptionist.

"I told myself a joke, as it turns out…I've never heard it before!" Bob tried to force the giggles to recede, but failed miserably. The receptionist, Brenda, as the name tag stated, didn't bother to hide the confusion she wore openly on her face.

"Can I help you Sir?"

"Um…Yes. I have a delivery for a Mr. Quinten."

"Please sign in and leave the package in receiving." She said in a monotone verse.

Sign in; sign in, Bob's mind raced as he tried to come up with a fake name. He smiled as he put the pen to the paper. The shrub still in his mind's eye, he wrote.

Gron, Ted

"Thank you, have a nice day!" Bob examined Brenda's expression for any sign of suspicion. When he was sure she was uninterested, he made his way back to the sweltering vehicle and waited, confident of his plan.

*****

A cold piercing stare is all he could manage. The letter addressed to him had over two hundred signatures and spanned four departments. His mind raced as he tried to make sense of it all. Mr. Quinten straightened his tie and took one more swig from his magic elixir in the frosted glass. Once more he focused on the words.

Mr.Quinten,

We are unsure if you are aware of the changes that have taken place this week in your company. The work environment we endure is highly unacceptable! We have no coffee, we have no office supplies, and the rolling blackouts are making our work space increasingly hot. On top off all of that, we have no 'Enter' keys on our keyboards. Many rodents wearing what appears to be a diaper will not let us open the cabinets or icebox in the break room. We have seen two supervisors leave, a toupee dangle, and a horrible stench is coming from the fern in the lobby. We cannot take it anymore. You have until Monday to fix it or we will be on strike.

He slammed the paper down on the table and slumped in his chair. A mix between anger and sadness drained him of any energy he had left. He knew what they were talking about. The blackouts affected him as well, and he had to send his receptionist to a coffee shop every morning this week. Another day or two like this and his company may never recover. The losses were astronomical, the worst they have ever been in his company and he may not see another million dollar month.

He stood, walking through the large corridor that separated him from the lowlife workers beneath his greedy Capitalistic thumb. Since the power outages, he had to walk to his receptionist's desk anytime he needed something.

"Laurie, could you go on a coffee run for me?"

"Sure thing Mr. Quinten."

The young blonde tugged her mini-skirt down to the appropriate level before standing eye to eye with the man, knowing full well her job depended on the condition of her legs and the amount of cloth covering them. She lifted her purse from the hook and slung it over her slender shoulder. A single memo fell from the top. Laurie slowly bent over to pick up the memo, giving the pig ample time to get an eyeful. She always did this with important memos. It softened the blow of bad news and gave her…um…job security.

"Mr. Quinten, a couple of items were delivered to you this morning, they are in receiving awaiting your approval." Laurie sneered as his line of sight never left the hem of her very mini-skirt.

"Thank you Laurie, I'll head over there now."

"You're welcome Sir, oh and will you be getting the usual today?"

"Fine, Fine, that will do."

The clinking of her high heels against the marble floor brought him out of his daze. He was reminded of how great his life was up until now. Fear of losing his company, brought renewed vigor to the tasks ahead. He slowly made his way down the stairs only letting his workers see his smile.

When he made it through the lobby to receiving, the overwhelming stench of the fern burned his nasal passages. They really do have it bad, don't they he thought. Well…I guess I'm glad it's not me.

Brenda gave him her biggest fake smile. "Good Morning Sir! A package was delivered by a Mr. Gron Ted. Oops…I mean Mr. Ted Gron. Also, a letter by a gentleman who claims to be Craig. I inspected his work I.D. and his real name is Conway. I'm not sure what that is about, but I took the letter for you anyway."

"Thank you Brenda."

"You're welcome sir. If there is anything thing else I can do for you just ask." Brenda once again slid a pseudo-smile his way, hoping he would notice.

"Fine fine, that will do!" Mr. Quinten took the package and the odd letter and neatly tucked it under his arm. He marched, executive style, back towards the shiny stairs.

Once out of earshot, Brenda's smile faded. "Have a heaping helping of fern, you asshole!" she mumbled through gritted teeth.

*****

The leather briefcase left tiny strips of debris among his office. After an hour of gnawing, Dribbles managed his stent of freedom. His large bushy tail flicked as his mind worked overtime. Then off into the wide world of office spaces he ventured. He ran under cubicles, and back into his previous workspace. Many cheers arose as everyone in the ten-cubicle radius caught glimpse of the mighty squirrel. To them, he was a hero, not a villain. He had slain the mighty Mr. Jefferson and they were thankful. The noise startled Dribbles, causing his pace to quicken by a leap or two. Finally, he found Mr. Quinten's storage locker. He immediately began stealing the tiny golf balls, hiding them in various hard to reach spaces. When he was all done, he headed out the back door. Sunlight and cool breeze ruffled his fur as he made his way back to the mighty Oak tree. As he climbed back up the branches and positioned himself, Conway sat down and smiled. His hand was already searching for the pack of cigarettes that dwelled deep in his pockets. Life was good!

*****

Mr. Quinten set the package down on his desk with a mighty thud and snatched the letter opener from the holder to his left. He held the sealed envelope up and touched the tip of his mini-sword to the paper. Then, everything went dark.

Darkness engulfed the room and noise filled the air. Something furry brushed his hand and quickly retreated across the desk. When the light came back on…his letter opener was gone.

Well that was annoying! He thought to himself as he ripped open the envelope and spilled the contents upon his desk. He felt the thin paper between his fingers and it just seemed to radiate bad news. He flipped it over and began to read.

Mr. Quinten,

As you may know, we are having a problem with our electricity.

"No shit buddy!" he stammered

As your...

Once again darkness, horrible scratchy sounds, and the occasional brush with furry annoyance replaced his pleasant working environment. The lights came flooding back into the room and the letter was turned upside down in his hands. Harsh thoughts replaced any moral responses to the situation he may have had. He thrust his body out of his chair and charged the door, more annoyed than he has ever been. He turned the brass knob and yelled as loud as he could to Laurie.

"FIRE SOMEONE. FIRE SOMEONE LAURIE AND DON'T SEND THEM A CHRISTMAS HAM! I EXPECT TO SEE TERMINATION PAPERS ON MY DESK IN AN HOUR!"

"Who should I fire Sir?"

"ANYONE! I DON'T CARE. FIRE SOMEONE UGLY!"

"Right away Sir!"

He relaxed deep in his chair and took a deep breath. He poured himself a drink and once again attempted to read the letter.

Mr. Quinten,

As you may know, we are having problems with our electricity. As your maintence man, I alone have the technical background to fix the problem for good. I will do so and save you thousands of dollars by preventing the worker strike I have heard so much about. I simply want a two dollar raise for my services.

Thank you,

Craig (Conway) Smith

P.S. Someone stole the batteries out of your flashlight.

Mr. Quinten flung the letter across the room and swiped the remaining stack of paperwork off his desk. He stood up and grabbed the back of the chair and flung it as well. It landed hard with a deafening crash. He spotted the package, sitting on the edge of the desk, half on and half off. He lifted it above his head, and stopped himself before hurling it as well. He slowly replaced it to its home and inhaled sharply. He could feel his heart pounding and his blood pressure rising.

I need to relax he thought. A quick game of golf, and I will be just fine. Everything will be just fine. He looked at the disaster he created on his precious golf course. His ball was nowhere to be seen, swallowed by the aftermath of an impatient man. He sighs and walks out of his office and into the lobby. He smiles at Laurie and makes his way to his storage locker to get a fresh supply of golf balls. He reaches in and feels the cold metal of the vastly empty locker. He attempts once more, and achieves the same results.

"SON OF A BITCH!"

The sound resonates with a boom through the entire building. Everyone knows that voice and trembles before it. Everywhere, everybody and everything was stopped. Dozens of eyes stare blankly at him as he walks among the crowd of shocked onlookers. He passes the reception desk in the lobby where Brenda smiles once more.

"Is everythin..."

"Nuh uh!"

He holds his hand up in front of her face, cutting her off mid-sentence. He marches on through the lobby and into the accounting department. One brave soul attempts once again.

"Good Mornin…"

"Nope!"

He holds his hand up once more and keeps walking. Now back on the top floor, he trudges back into his office and grabs a single item. He stares only at the tiles as he approaches Laurie's desk. She puzzles at the sight of this, but knows better to ask.

"Give Conway a raise."

"Right away Sir!"

He says nothing else as he takes the stairs two at a time and makes his way back to the storage locker. Quiet whispers can be heard among the workers as they ponder the events that they are witnessing. Fear, confusion, and the occasional excitement passed for emotions among them.

Mr. Quinten stared calmly at the large locker analyzing it. Finally he pulled the golf club out from under his arm and beat it over and over again. Loud crippling sounds from metal on metal and words not yet defined by Webster's Dictionary was all the noise to be heard. After five grueling minutes, the golf club threw in the towel and bowed out. The head, hanging on for dear life, rested near the handle.

He walked, with a smile on his face, past Brenda.

"Good Morning Brenda."

"Good Morning sir."

She didn't bother to muster a smile this time, letting the confusion show. He hummed a happy hum while making his way back to his office. Once there, he laid the battered putter to rest among the golf course graveyard he created. Back on track, he lifted the package and tore into the brown paper surrounding it.

Seven black and white photos were neatly bunched up inside. Pictures of squirrels, big and small stared up at him. Some were stealing office supplies, and others were stealing keys off of keyboards. One in particular shocked him, a picture of a squirrel terrorizing poor Mr. Jefferson in the elevator. A letter with no signature lay beneath

I know what is happening here and I have the power to stop it. Workers are going to strike and investors will hear about it. You will lose everything. I want two million dollars. I want this by Monday or it will get worse. I will be watching!

He stood and ran. He ran to Laurie and slid the paper in front of her. He puffed and puffed for oxygen, and was finally able to speak.

"He's here! Call security!"

*****

Jonathan kept his feet high up on the chair. He never moved and hardly spoke. The guard shack was the easiest job in the company, but with mediocrity comes low pay. He didn't mind though, he spent his days checking work badges and watching television. His favorite show just started and he didn't want to miss anything, but that's how it goes. His arch nemesis, Mr. Quinten, bringer of work and all things unholy and minimum wage; just set off his radio. "Security...krrr...krrr." Jonathan stretched his arm to his waist to retrieve the radio that remained at his hip. He was worried he may have to move his legs to reach it, but was relieved when his thumb bumped the clasp.

"This is security."

"Lock down the parking lot and search the area. We have a vandal on the loose."

"Yes Sir. I will snoop around."

The theme song was just winding down when he decided to let his feet touch the concrete. He hit the switch that lowered the flimsy aluminum arm across the exit. He grabbed his flashlight and mace and slowly made his way across the parking lot. It's times like this that I hate my job he thinks. He glances back at the flimsy arm and notices it bowing in the middle. The wind makes mini waves and an ominous splooshing sound radiates from it. Yea…that will stop them. Two tons of steel will hit that and stop in an instant. The criminals will get out and hold their head between their hands and say "I would have been fine if someone didn't deploy the aluminum arm of death."

If that doesn't do the trick, certainly a security guard that weighs a hundred and twenty pounds, and reaches the enormous height of five foot six, armed with a flashlight and mace will thwart any attempts to cause mischief. Jonathan let his mind drift as he shined the light in every vehicle looking for intruders. A couple taking a long lunch break passed their work I.D.'s to him and he moved on. Everything seemed very quiet. As he passed the entrance to the office, he decided ten minutes of walking was all he could handle comfortable. He sat down on the sidewalk and looked around. Nothing out of the ordinary struck his fancy.

The birds and squirrels played a game of hide and seek. The bee's were hard at work spreading pollen here and there. Even the employees who took a late lunch settled back inside. Everything seemed perfectly…well, boring. Jonathan noticed the maintence man sitting down and staring intently at the oak tree, waiting for it to speak or talk or something.

"You there! Do you have some I.D.?"

Craig just smiled and pulled out his wallet.

"You know I do Jonathan. Who let you out of your box?"

"Ha-ha, very funny. I was sent on a very important mission to annoy you."

Craig handed him a cigarette and lit one himself.

"Making you earn your buck fifty are they?"

"They are convinced some maniac is stalking the company."

"I have found no sign of life out here, besides you that is."

Craig stared hopefully at Dribbles. If he chose this particular moment to make a cameo, than their game of cat and mouse would have to come to an end.

"Well...No time like the present. I'm off to search the back row. Hopefully, I can still catch the last ten minutes of my show."

"Wow, you really do have it bad, don't you?"

"Bite me Conway!"

Craig watched the odd little guard bounce along the parking lot shining beam after beam into cars.

*****

Bob never saw it coming. He was so fixated on what was happening inside that he forgot to pay attention. Three cars down a young man was closing in on him with his flashlight. After about five minutes, the tapping on the glass brought his attention back to the outside world. Bob slowly rolled his window down and stared at the security guard.

"Do you have your I.D. Sir?"

"I'm sure I have it here somewhere."

Bob searched his glove-box, looked under his seat, and even pulled the visor down and went through the paperwork. He was busted and he knew it.

"Well…Do you have it or don't you?"

"I'm sorry, I guess I lost it."

"Of course you did Sir."

Jonathan pulled the ugly green notepad from his pocket and produced an ink-pen. "What's your name sir?"

Thinking quick Bob came up with another fake identity. Remembering the roster of names he would send emails out for, he chose one at random.

"Jonathan Carr."

The security guard did not look amused. He simply tapped his name tag and looked at him dumbfounded.

"Nice try Sir, but there is only one Jonathan Carr here and he looks dashing in his uniform!"

"If I can't verify that you are here for work, you will be escorted to jail, so cut the crap and tell me your name!"

The loud voice caused him to drop his notepad. From behind him came the squelch of Conway.

"He's with me! He's the new maintence man. I told him to keep an eye on the second floor and let me know when the power goes out so I can flip the breaker."

Jonathan stared once more at poor Bob and then looked back at Craig.

"He's a weird one, isn't he? Make sure he has a badge by Monday, understand?"

Craig shook his head and watched Jonathan hurry off towards his guard shack. His show is nearing the end, so it would be unlikely to see him again.

Conway tapped on Bob's window, causing his panic to rise once again.

"Don't worry, I'm not here to cause you trouble."

"Thank you!" Bob sighed uneasily and softened his stiff body.

"I know it was you that has been releasing those squirrels."

"I'm afraid I don't know what you are talking about Sir!"

"Of course you don't! I just wanted to thank you. Every since you have arrived, my job has been so much more enjoyable. Now leave, before you are spotted again. They know you are here."

Craig watched the mini-van make it out of the parking lot and into the highway. His exhaust leaving evidence of foul play, but, he will never tell!

Operation Extermination

Cody Toye

The black Firebird rolled down the highway exceeding ninety miles per hour. The blue and red lights colored the day. Seven of New York's finest police-man was in hot pursuit, armed with the booming siren of justice; they closed in on the maniac. As the dotted yellow lines started to blur, they watched in horror as the sports car darted back and forth into oncoming traffic. A rather large delivery truck bumped the curb and rolled into the grass. Smoke and dirt rose high into the air and directly attacked the officer's window. Now blind, he had no choice. Officer Ace Bradley pulled the hefty shotgun from the holder behind his partners back. As he stuck his head out of the window and took aim, the constant blaring of car horns reminded him of the danger he was putting innocent bystanders in. He has only one chance to get it right, only one bullet to stop this deranged criminal. The bullet disappeared into the chamber as he pulled down on the pump action Shot gun.

Jonathan Carr thought he was watching his favorite show in surround sound; it took only a moment longer to notice the large van idling at the security gate. Always when I get to the best part! He thinks to himself. The enormous plastic bug hinged to the roof was a dead giveaway that this was indeed the exterminator, but that wasn't the point. He had to miss the ending; he had to pull his feet off of the counter and stand-up. It's Saturday for Christ sake.

"Do you have an I.D. buddy?"

"You have got to be kidding me! Do you not see the large dead bug?"

The man slaps the plastic insect, making a hollow thud ring out.

"Do I look like I have a sense of humor Sir? No I.D. No entrance." Jonathan pulls off the best monotone smirk to match the voice.

After a long irritating silence, the man passes a shiny identification card through the window. Jonathan looks it over and hands it back.

"Carries Kill Center. Are you Carrie?"

"Do I look like Carrie?"

"Looks can be deceiving sir…Where is Carrie?"

"How the hell should I know?"

"Because you work for her…or you are her, which is it?"

"I don't have time for this shit. Are you going to let me in?"

"Fine, but I am watching you!"

Jonathan smashes the large red button, making the flimsy aluminum arm start to rise. The man starts mouthing words through his window, but nothing could be heard through the glass. Out of sheer curiosity he sticks his head back out and stares at Carrie.

"What was that?"

"I said...Officer Ace Bradley misses the tire and the Firebird gets away!"

The tires squelch, propelling the large van into the parking lot at tremendous speeds.

"YOU ASSHOLE!"

A defeated sigh escaped him, as he sat back down and propped his feet up on the counter, his attention was back on the small black and white television set. Life was good...almost. The man in the magic box made an announcement that caused a shudder to radiate through his spine.

"Hi kids. It is now time for your favorite cuddly bear. Welcome to Big Bear Hour!"

"SON OF A BITCH!"

*****

Bob paced the floor of his lavish hotel room, not sure how to act. For days, he sat in the sweltering van, watching with glee as the corporate giant felt the sting of his vengeance. One department at a time, Dribbles led them to victory. His moment was near, he could feel it. He could feel it and squeeze his fat fist around it. Then…then a rent-a-cop armed with a minimum wage attitude and a cheap walkie-talkie forced him to leave. His babies were still in there, trapped like a common rodents. He needed to get them out, today was the day! They shouldn't be in there; they will be hunted by a fat man with poison gas.

His pace picked up as the terrible thoughts drilled into his brain. Looking around the room in disgust, he longed for the nasty heat and foul smell of his van. The large television seemed to mock him from a distant, threatening an hour of enjoyment upon him. Out of curiosity, he gave in.

As the television set flipped on, he was enthusiastically greeted by the warm glow of a blue screen. Sound and picture soon followed suit. They were running a documentary on squirrel hibernation patterns, no wait…on squirrel fatalities during winter.

"Prey for Spring is brought to you by…"

~ 137 ~

Bob clicked the nasty devise off in horror, and continued to pace. He envisioned squirrels falling from the ceiling by the dozens, their diapers soiled as the nerve gas took effect. He imagined Dribbles running through the ventilation system one hop at a time, just to have an ugly head pop up and stop him in his tracks. "Where do you think you're going little fella? Mwahaha…"

Bob shook his head and willed the images away. He sat down on the edge of the king sized bed and placed his hands on his chin. I have got to get my mind straight. He thought to himself. He stared out the window for about ten minutes, taking in the view of Q.J. Enterprises across the street, before noticing the old Oak radio next to the bed. Why not? A little music would do me some good.

With a gentle click he found a station that seemed to satisfy him.

"91.3 NUTZ we're nuts for music. Up next is Alvin and the Chipmunks!"

Bob pulled the radio, plug and all, and chunked it across the room. The warm feeling of insanity started to flood his body and small chuckles tried to escape. In a panic, he throws his keys in his pocket and heads for the door. I need some air! He thinks.

*****

The van pulled into the parking spot with considerable ease. The whole place looked like a ghost town, sans the broken glass and boarded up windows. No…this ghost town had a gold encrusted mansion, infested with rodents. The man slapped the van into park and exited the vehicle. With a tug, he adjusted his coveralls and opened the back doors. With so many weapons to choose from, there was a slight delay in his actions. Finally, he lifted the magic wand attached to the pump and palmed three cans of Kill All Can Grenades. He felt around behind his toolbox until he bumped into the breathing apparatus. With a moment of struggle, the man fastened it into place, feeling like a soldier about to wade through a fog of Mustard gas.

He could hear his inhalations and smell the masks pungent odor. Through foggy plexi-glass, he watched for any sign of life. The long metal tip gleamed as it gracefully moved in a semi-circular motion in front of him. Thick fog came rolling out, coating the exterior of the doors. He watched as several crickets twitched in pain; he never understood their true purpose. He marched a soldier's march, spreading death among the insect world. One wall at a time, he started securing the perimeter. Thus blocking any attempts of escape from his foes. As he made his way around the last corner, he felt two beady eyes staring at him from the huge Oak tree.

His hand slowly reached to his belt, feeling the cold metal of a Can Grenade. His fist wrapped around it, making it ready for battle. He crept towards the tree not knowing what to expect. The light clicking of an acorn rolling down the rain gutter caused him to jump and turn his head. Another acorn followed by another echoed through the cheap aluminum pipes. Then, out of the corner of his eye, he caught sight of a brown blur hopping on the roof of the corporation. "Clever little shit, aren't you?"

With the acorns pitter-patter still ringing in his ears, he pulled the pin and chunked the grenade at the tree branch. He watched it bounce off and land non-chalantly onto the metal. He had seen it land and heard it roll, and waited for the monstrous cloud to cover the roof. Instead, all he heard was an even louder clank from the rain gutter. To his horror, the can came rolling out and stopped only a yard from him. His vision started to blur as the can continued to spew toxic fumes into the air. Through the fog and milky goggles, a bushy tail flicked and disappeared. Not missing a beat, the man shouldered his way through the doorway and took chase. Dribbles ran across the light fixtures and hopped onto support beams, but the masked man stayed only a step behind him.

*****

Spoon after spoonful went into Jonathan's mouth. Milk dribbled down his chin and the internal crunch of Cheerios rang in his ears. Loud heinous laughter erupted and his gaping mouth showed the world how skilled he was at chewing up his breakfast. His body rocked back and forth as he waited patiently to see the untimely death of the roadrunner. The fuse fizzled and the coyote was sent into a boulder at a tremendous rate of speed. Jonathan exploded with laughter once more. You would think he would start buying his products elsewhere wouldn't you? He chuckled to himself. The honking of the bird was abruptly interrupted by the honking of a Buick Sedan. Now what?

Jonathan slowly turned towards the window intent on giving that fat slob a piece of his mind. To his surprise, the part of the hideous van was being played by a quaint Buick. The smiling face of his longtime friend startled him.

"Well what do we have here? You know I can't let you in on a Saturday without authorization Craig."

"I need to get in there. It is very important that you let me in."

Jonathan rolled this over in his mind for a minute or two and came up with an astute answer

"No!"

"What do you mean no? I have to."

"Why is that? What is so important that you are willing to risk my job over?"

"Do you want me to level with you?"

"That would be the only way to gain entry…and it better be good too, I have a feeling the coyote is going to win this time. I have been waiting years for that. If I miss it, so help me…"

Craig couldn't help but like a man who centered his life around such silliness

"Do you like your job Jonathan? Would you like a raise? Better yet, how would you like it if you had to work for your money?"

"BITE YOUR TONGUE!"

"Yea, now I have your full attention."

"Do you remember the squirrels that have been causing problems?"

"Yes. The exterminator is here right now to take care of it. What about them?"

"Do you know what will happen if he kills them?"

"Everything will be back to normal. Is there a point to this?"

Craig felt like he was talking to a toddler. He bit his lip in frustration and inhaled deeply.

"Let me throw this out there for you. Things will go back to normal, except..."

"Except what? Come on Craig spit it out!"

"Mr. Quinten will have to make up the losses by cutting payroll. If he does that, Maintence and Security will be the first to be let go. We are the expendable ones. Then poor little Jonathan Carr will have to earn his keep. You will have to do more than watch television for a living!"

Jonathan could feel his chest tighten at the thought.

"What happens if the squirrels survive?"

Craig smiled and relaxed his body deep into his seat; he knew this would reel him in, hook, line, and sinker.

"Then everyone goes on strike. Mr. Quinten will need crowd control from security, and I will have to fix anything the mob breaks. This is when you can negotiate a raise."

"You are a twisted little man. But I think you are a brilliant twisted little man! Go get'em!"

Jonathan smashed the button for the second time and watched the arm slowly rise. Just as the Buick began to pull forward, Jonathan stuck his head back through the window.

"Bring me back some chips would ya?"

"You got it buddy!"

*****

"Would you like a sandwich, a salad, or a flatbread today?" Bob stared at the teen, unaware of how the store operated. So many questions, not enough answers. He bit his bottom lip and started to sweat profusely. The blonde's impatience and the ever growing crowd made concentration a mere fairy-tale. In college, Bob would study long and hard, never stopping until he had the right answer. What was the right answer? Could it be A? How about C? The answer was B, nine times out of ten it was B.

He could hear the murmurs coming from behind him, attacking him, and leaving nasty red mental bumps as they inserted their indignant stingers deep into his memory. The cashier's gaze was a heat sinking missile, Bob's pupils, the victim of a villainous plot of destruction. He could feel the heat radiating off of the florescent lights, and smell the fear pouring out of himself. How can she do this to me? The bitch! A pop quiz right in middle of public, she is the devil.

"Sir?"

"C-c-can you repeat the question?"

A puzzled look crossed the pretty face of the teen, but anxious to move things along, she immediately complied.

"Would you like a sandwich, a salad, or a flatbread today?"

"B THE ANWSER IS B! AM I RIGHT?"

"Um…sure"

Bob watched as the young lady turned and grabbed a salad bowl from the toaster behind her. As she adjusted her gloves, routine took hold.

"What kind of salad would you like?"

She immediately covered her mouth, knowing full well the damage she has just caused. To her relief, Bob started spouting off the list of ingredients he would like.

"I would like Lettuce, Walnuts, Pecans, Almonds, Cashews, and Ranch dressing please."

"Sorry sir, we don't carry those."

Devastation sprinkled with confusion sank in. Until now, his thoughts were on poor Dribbles and the squad of minions fighting a losing battle. Unaware of what he said, he tried to remain calm. Deep inside the pit of his stomach he could feel madness rising.

"I'm sorry, what don't you have Ma'am?"

"Nuts."

"I AM NOT!" at her blank stare, he realized she was not questioning his sanity, but that they didn't serve nuts. "THERE ARE DOZENS OF SQUIRRELS UNDER MY CONTROL RUNNING AMUCK. DO THEY HAVE THE OPPORTUNITY TO EAT A SALAD? DID YOU ASK THEM IF THEY WANTED A FLATBREAD? NO. RIGHT NOW THEY NEED A DIAPER CHANGE AND FED BEFORE THEY CAN CONTINUE TO TEAR DOWN CORPORATE AMERICA AND YOU ARE GOING TO INFORM ME THAT

THEIR MISSION WILL FAIL BECAUSE YOU DO NOT HAVE THE INGREDIENTS NEEDED TO MAKE A SIMPLE SALAD. "

His chest caved in and expanded as he inhaled deeply. He saw a look of terror on the poor girls face and watched her back slowly towards the door. Once she disappeared, a simple thought occurred to him. I'm losing it! I need to get them out of there right now before I cause any more trouble. He heard a small click and a deep voice came over the intercom system.

"Security Check"

"Shit!"

*****

Dribbles could feel the man's stare and hear the steady Clack of his shoes beating around behind him. His balance was impeccable as he jumped from pipe to pipe to avoid the man's rage. The florescent lights swayed to and fro as he stopped dead center to breathe. The man tried to concentrate on his furry nemesis, but could not get his eyes to focus properly. In place of the squirrel, danced red dots before his pupils. The nozzle of his sprayer aimed high as the stainless steel gleamed mockingly. Certain death came to all who were unlucky enough to catch a glimpse of that wand.

Like a deer in a trance, caught in the high beams on a desolate highway, Dribbles could not break away from his stare-down. The fat finger of the city's most efficient killer slowly started to squeeze the trigger. Before the toxic cloud could spew out, the lights went out.

The spell now broken, Dribbles took off down the lights and across the pipes. The man had to go by sound alone, but could pinpoint the general location of the foul beast. One foot in front of the other, he followed the hollow echo of metal on metal as the lights collided into each other. His sprayer led the way, spilling toxins towards any unidentified sound. A thick fog started filling the dark room; another ten minutes and anything that breathes would suffer a cruel fate. He knew he had him, only one way in and one way out. The man laughs as the filter on his mask prevents poison from entering his lungs. His body slowly backs to the only exit in the room, blocking it completely. It was now simply a waiting game and he was still on the clock. After only a few minutes, he could hear the scratching on the marble floor as his arch-nemesis attempted to make a run for it. The man pulled the pin and chunked the Can-Grenade towards the ominous sound, hoping to hear the nasty thud of metal on meat.

The can rolled, screeching along the marble. An audible hiss echoed as its contents spilled out of the nozzle. A direct miss! The man's eyes strained to focus in the vast darkness. The scratching became louder, to almost deafening proportions. A tiny blur of brown fur became visible as he came face to face with his enemy for the first time. Only one of them was getting out of this room. A strange sensation came over the man, one he never expected. Large ugly dots covered his eye-sight; searing pain seemed to grow from directly underneath his cranium. His body became weak, then completely surrendered. The boom of the fat body collapsing was heard all the way at the guard shack.

*****

The hotel blinds were split apart once more as Bob's eye peered across the street at Q.J. Enterprises. To his surprise, another vehicle was parked in the lavish parking lot. He watched Conway the maintence man come walking out of the side entrance, carrying a large Crescent Wrench. Horror swelled deep inside, as violent thoughts plagued him. Bob could picture the brute swinging with all his might at his furry buddies, making contact with a horrible thud. Squirrels would fly through the air, only to land unconscious across the room. What kind of monster would do such a thing?

Bobs pace quickened. For over ten minutes now, he has been walking back and forth in front of the window uncertain of what to do. A thought occurred to him, who's side is he on? Memories of his close call had him doubting himself. Is he a friend or is he a monster?

He closed his eyes and replayed it over again in his mind.

"If I can't verify that you are here for work, you will be escorted to jail, so cut the crap and tell me your name!"

"He's with me! He's the new maintenance man. I told him to keep an eye on the second floor and let me know when the power goes out so I can flip the breaker."

"Make sure he has a badge by Monday, understand?"

Conway tapped on Bob's window, causing his panic to rise once again. "Don't worry, I'm not here to cause you trouble."

"Thank you!" Bob sighed uneasily and softened his stiff body.

"I know it was you that has been releasing those squirrels."

"I'm afraid I don't know what you are talking about Sir!"

"Of course you don't! I just wanted to thank you. Every since you have arrived, my job has been so much more enjoyable. Now leave, before you are spotted again. They know you are here."

Bob shook away the memory now certain of one thing…they needed his help. He snatched his sunglasses and threw his wallet in his pocket. Excitement and energy seemed to fill him to the core; he may get them out yet!

*****

Craig watched as the man blocked the only exit out of Q.J. Enterprises. He heard the Can-Grenade hit and slide across the marble floor. Time was limited. He inhaled deeply, taking the last drag off of his cigarette before littering the parking lot with the used butt. The orange glow of the tip sparked and expanded into many bits as it collided with the pavement.

He knew what he had to do, but it went against everything he believed in. On one hand, it is very inhumane to land a forceful blow to the back of someone's head. On the other, he has grown to love those little guys, especially the tree hugger that has made his job so simple these last few days. If the exterminator kills him then life will return to normal. I will have to use these blasted tools and pretend like I know what the hell I'm doing! Deep in thought, Craig's hand slides to the Crescent Wrench on his tool belt. He feels the cold metal in his hand as he hoists it out of its home.

"What the hell is this Chompy-Thingy McBob anyways? I may not know how to use it, but I sure know how to swing it!" He mumbles under his breath as he rears back for the attack. With all of his might, he swings at the back of the man's head. The cold steel connects with flesh and nothing happens. For a good minute solid, Craig watched the man stand his ground. Fear creeps up on him like a shadow in the night.

Any minute he will turn around and attack me. He will say something like...

"Did you think that silly little Chompy-Thingy McBob could stop me? Hahaha I am immune to Chompy-Thingy McBobs and now you will pay!"

His hand reaches back to his tool belt, feeling for anything that would make a good back up weapon. The largest item left is a simple flathead screwdriver. Without hesitation, he draws the mammoth weapon out of its makeshift sheath and wields it like a true knight. The light reflects off of a solid twelve inches of chrome, building confidence at the task ahead. His knuckles turn white as the strength of his grip increases.

"SCREW YOU!"

He closed his eyes and held his breathe waiting for the battle to begin. A loud thump took the place of the death blow he was waiting for. When he opened his eyes, the man lay upon the marble, victim of Craig the Dragon-Slayer. An audible oomph came cascading out of the brave man, as he tried to regain the normalcy of his heartbeat. He watched with delight as Dribbles led the squirrel army out of the gas chamber and into the warmth of the day. A small victory for the worker bees, but a victory none the less!

*****

Bob darted across the busy freeway, ignoring the honks and cursing radiating from oncoming traffic. With so much at stake, nothing would stop him. As he passed the arch way and made his way towards the guard shack, his body began to tremble. Too many years sitting behind a desk had made him weak, a blob of a man who, up until now avoided physical exertion at all costs. But this was important Damn it! He trudged on, forcing his body to bow to his will. He finally made it to the shack when a voice reminded him where he was.

"Whoa there buddy. It's Saturday. I can't let you in there"

Bob stared at the scrawny man wishing his head would explode.

"Humph. Humph. I gotta…humph"

"You gotta lay off of the cheeseburgers, that's what you got to do. I told you already, no one is allowed in there today."

"It's an emergency. I have to get in or else…"

"Or else what? Or else your squirrels will die?"

Bob stood in shocked silence. For the first time all day, his brain didn't want to respond to the situation at hand.

"Listen, pal personally I'm with you. Down with the man and all of that jazz, but I can't risk letting you in. If you get caught then it's my ass and I intend on getting paid to watch the road-runner meet his demise."

"How can I save them then? What about Dribbles, What about the exterminator? What about…"

"It's all taken care of. Come Monday morning, Mr. Quinten will have a strike on his hands."

"How do you know this? Right now there could be…"

"Shh…just trust me, everything will work out."

It was at that particular moment that Bob heard the loud thump and watched his minions escape with their lives. Everything did work out. This guard is a genius!

"I will see you Monday then?"

Merchant of Death

Cody Toye

The needle tore deep into the plastic wrapper leaving the slightest pinhole lingering for evidence. Cecil Smiled devilishly and stared at his remaining product. The ten o'clock news ran another special on the heinous crimes plaguing Northwest Arkansas, this time labeling him the "Merchant of Death."

I'm the Merchant of Death? This thought amused the tiny man. A hellish cackle escaped his lips and continued to illuminate his madness. As he finished injecting the last of tomorrow's product, he heard the announcement that ten more were found dead today, bringing the death toll to eighty-two. This set him off once again. Through the spray of spittle and the booming laugh, he was able to correct the old tube television set and inform it that the death toll was actually one hundred and three.

*****

The sun beat down on the old Ford van, reflecting the bright yellow paint. The multitude of colored dots offset the décor nicely. Sprinkle Ice Cream was open for business once more and what a day it would be! The heat index called for a record high and was predicting a scorching one hundred and eight, a perfect day for his ice cream truck. Cecil cringed at the sound of the rusty hinges of the back doors creaking open. As he loaded the last of his freight into the Nelson freezer, he placed his "special product" to the far left making it easy to dispense at will. With one more walk around, he was ready to start his day. The lyrical hum of "Colonel Bogey's March" filled the summer air. With perked interest, dozens of kids rounded the corner and jumped over the hedge. The younger group simply dropped what they were doing and started bouncing up and down. The "Ice cream dance" as he came to refer to it over the years, brought streams of adults with fistfuls of money out into the heat.

One by one, Cecil handed out cones, sandwiches, and fruity colorful ice pops. A devilish grin never left his face as he pulled from the special inventory and randomly handed them out. He knew he was nothing more than a social disease, a killer of children tall and small, yet he somehow felt at ease ridding the world of the overfed spoiled American children. Visions of his childhood plagued him. Little Cecil, only eight years old, watched from the steps of the orphanage as spoiled brats bought gobs of ice cream from the Good Humor truck and mockingly ate it in front of him. Some of the even meaner children went as far as throwing the half- eaten ice cream at him, hoping to see it splatter moments before he could catch it. Poor Cecil! Who's laughing now? A stifled giggle caught in his throat, creating a nasty gurgling sound to splash out.

*****

Mary Calhoon peered through the blinds at the bright van. After a month and a half, she finally gave in and let her little girl get ice cream. She still didn't trust him, something about the man behind the steering wheel still creeped her out. Her eyes remained glued on her little girl as she pulled the ice cream cone from the man's hand and bounced happily across the street towards her mommy. Her red hair glimmered in the sunlight as her pigtails raised and lowered in the most amusing fashion. A warm feeling spread deep in Mary's stomach, the love for her burned constantly. Her little girl was growing up, maybe just a little too fast.

"Look mommy, look what I got!" Mary stared at the freckled face and giggled as she wiggled her little nose. "Look mommy it's a Nucky Broyale." This set her off again, uncontrollable laughter radiated from the woman and left little Annie confused. "You're so cute, come here you!" With one swift movement, Annie was lifted high into the air and pulled tightly against her mother's chest in a tight embrace.

"Careful, mommy, you'll squish my ice cream."

"Okay, okay, run along and eat it before it melts"

An innocent little grin spread below the freckles as she stared at her mommy

"A Nucky Broyale puddle?"

"That's right dear, a Nutty Royal puddle."

She watched as her only daughter galloped up the stairs and unwrap the wrath of Cecil…The Merchant of Death.

*****

The money wasn't important to him; however, three hundred dollars profit for a day's work wasn't bad at all. He eagerly backed the large van into the garage and with a nasty clunk he killed the engine. He was a private man, an outcast to society, the nameless face known simply as the ice cream man. To his knowledge no one ever questioned him. They didn't care where he got the vehicle, what company he worked for, or even if he had a driver's license. Never did they want to know if he was convicted of any sex crimes or if he was a drunk. Nope…they simply accepted the fact that he exists. A total stranger in mist consented to interact with their children. That is why they must pay, the ignorance and greed that has become so celebrated in this nation is nothing more than a festering disease rapidly consuming every single neighborhood in America. I have the cure; I alone can stop it before it is too late.

The grimace of insanity once again decorated his face. He slowly walked to the back of the van and effortlessly lifted the case of ice cream cones. With a steady echo, he made his way through the garage. The door squeaked as he entered the living room, the smell of moldering pizza attacked his nostrils forcing him to recoil. The small floral loveseat, now stained from sweat and week old pizza sauce, still held a perfect imprint of his large ass. He cringed at the sound of rusty metal being forced together, but still felt the need to kick up his feet and relax.

The small brown tray held the needles and the black tray held the sin aid. All he needed was the needles for now, the needles and the small vile he kept stashed in the nightstand. He slid it open and blindly let his fingers glide back and forth until it bumped something cold and hard. With little thought, he gripped the vile and brought to his lap. As he inserted the needle deep into the liquid, he stared at the rapidly melting box of ice cream sitting next to him.

"Patience, patience…you'll get what's coming to you, but first I will get what's coming to me. Hehe he hehe. Hahaha." The sinister laugh was cut short by the sharp inhalation of air. His eyes lolled back as he felt the sting of the needle punching through his skin.

*****

Mary Calhoon felt the clammy skin of her precious daughter. The heat began to fade from her body. The drips of medicine and the horrible sounds of the doctor's voices boomed into the deepest recesses of her mind. The gentle humming of the florescent lights seemed to scream in anger as the reality hit her. My baby girl is gonna die. Fat streams of tears came flooding down her cheeks as she tilted her head in silent prayer. Mary Calhoon has been in the operating room for twelve hours. Twelve hours of praying, twelve hours of feeling her heart skip a beat every time the green vertical line spiked and tried to go flat. Every now and again, a sweet voice would permeate the vastness of her mind.

"It was him mommy. It was the Nucky Broyal." The words would linger like a foul meal at a cheap drive through.

Little Annie sits straight up. Red pigtails and freckles splashed upon her nose as she smiled. With a quick hop and a gentle tap of her little feet connecting with the bright floor, she would leap upon mommy's lap and throw her little arms around her neck. Her bright piercing gaze would connect and tug with Mary's heart. Like a puppet, Annie could control the very strings to her soul. Her sweet breathe would tickle as she spoke

"Don't be sad mommy. Don't be sad."

"GET REVENGE, KILL THE BASTARD."

The anguish screams of her little girl's death registers in her mind as it fades into a barrage of beeps. Mary Calhoon grabs her chest, soaked in sweat and weak from the many sleepless nights. She fumbles to ease the noise croaking from the alarm clock and breaks down. Sweat and tears stain her nightgown as she no more than rolls to her side and curls her knees to her chest. "I will baby, Mommy will make it right." She mumbles to herself.

*****

Cecil squirmed in his chair, trying to squeeze some sort of comfort out of the barstool. The bartender just rolls his eyes as he fills the mug with "premium" as the man puts it. He was used to Cecil though, He watched the man come in every Friday wearing the same dingy shirt. Pit-stains and what looked to be vomit was always caked on the front. Between the foul odor and the nasty clothing, he wondered why he even bothered to seek out a ladies company. They never came. Never would anyone of the opposite sex even bother to glance in his direction. Wonder why? He smiled at his own dumb joke as he handed the mug to the man.

He slid the money from the counter into his hand and placed it in the register. His goal was not to say a word, rather move away as quick as possible.

"One more please." A voice rang out

The bartender almost dropped to his knees as he watched the foxy red-head sit next to Cecil and smile. She was wearing a rather small black miniskirt and something that was neither shirt nor bandana around her large chest. He poured another beer and just watched from a distance, floored by the fact that Cecil could attract such a beauty. "Guess his patience paid for once."

They whispered back and forth for about an hour before she started getting real flirty with him. Her hand rested upon his knee and her bright red lipstick tried to smear as she spoke softly into his ear. Not a whole lot was audible to the bartender, but the conversation shifted to his crummy ice cream truck. He caught little bits of this and that and pieced it together like an erotic jig-saw puzzle.

"Take her for a ride in your truck?" I know what that means you lucky son of a bitch.

He snickered to himself and pondered the true meaning of life. Divorced for thirteen years and a woman like that never once looked at him. "And I have a respectable job! Ice Cream man...pfft." He gestured a dismissive gesture as his thought shifted. Cecil and the pin up girl slowly walked towards the night. The bartender watched her little ass wiggle as she made her way through the door with Cecil the repulsive.

*****

The sprinklers churned in unison on Marvin Street. As far as the eyes could see, arcs of water collided with the children. The happy noise of a summer's day blanketed the entire neighborhood. The children ran and giggled through the water, only stopping because something of greater interest slowly made its way down the street.

"ICE CREAM MAN!"

Dozens of children, dripping wet, started chasing the sweet sounds of desert. The sun reflected off of the yellow décor as it stopped at the end of the road and roughly idled. They gathered in masses for the treasured deserts, listening to Colonel Bogey's March. Something was different this time though. The kids knew it, but so did the hordes of adults peering through their mini-blinds. The news of little Annie made the front page and all the parents are concerned.

They watched curiously as the children circled the van. In place of the horrible man was an attractive red-head clutching the steering wheel. A sigh of relief washed over many, knowing the ice cream man was no more. Then, to their surprise, she left. The red-headed woman simply slammed her door with a loud clank and started walking up the street. She could hear the children screaming and crying, but chose to ignore the "Ice Cream Dance."

With the music still blaring and the children throwing tantrums, one adult braved the crowd to see what was happening. As he crawled into the van, the smell of blood filled his nose. Something was not right indeed!

It was only after he pulled open the Nelson freezer that he called the cops. White as a ghost he proceeded to relive the experience to the office that arrived on the scene. Officer Johnson slowly pulled open the deep freezer, certain that the rattled adult didn't see what he thought he did. It creaked open slowly exposing the contents inside. The freezer was void of any frozen desert, but instead contained thirty "flavors" of human remains. A bloody arm, head, finger, and much more were crammed into it. Blood and gore was splashed all over the inside.

Officer Johnson started moving the parts this way and that, trying to struggle with finding all the parts to the victim. His hand wrapped around Cecil's Penis. Cold and flaccid, it flopped about in his knuckles like a dead fish on a hot day. He flat lost it.

The brave officer thrust his head out the window and lost every bit of food he digested that day. He was certain he also lost yesterdays as well. He sat in the van, sweaty and ill, staring at the member. Sewed into the penis with black thread was a picture of a little red-head girl. Freckles and bright happy eyes seemed very out of place in such a gruesome crime scene. As he flipped the photo over, a sentence written in the victim's blood was etched. Barely able to read it, Officer Johnson spoke the words out loud

"Mommy got him baby."

Logged Off

Cody Toye

Sparkle_Kitty has joined the chat

DarkThunder92 has joined the chat

DarkThunder92: I was wondering when I was gonna see you.

Sparkle_Kitty: Why did you miss me? ;)

DarkThunder92: Of course I did

DarkThunder92: -playfully pokes Sparkle-

Unknown Prey has joined the chat

Sparkle_Kitty: -giggles-

Sparkle_Kitty: I was havin a bit of a problem today, kept me offline for a bit

Sparkle_Kitty: -pouts-

DarkThunder92: Is okay –smiles- what was the problem?

Unknown Prey: Hello

Sparkle_Kitty: It was Ryan again, he was taken into custody for bringing knife to school

Sparkle_Kitty: Hi Prey

DarkThunder92: Hi Unknown

DarkThunder92: Ryan? I'm sorry but your brother is a bit crazy

Sparkle_Kitty: I know he is, but I'm worried about him.

Sparkle_Kitty: (seriously, he cuts himself sometimes)

Unknown Prey: -Sits in corner and twiddles thumbs-

DarkThunder92: Im sorry to hear that.

DarkThunder92: What are you gonna do?

Unknown Prey: hi all…-waves-

Sparkle_Kitty: Hi Prey, we are having important conversation, please be quiet

Unknown Prey: :(

Sparkle_Kitty: What can I do? I went to see him behind bars this morning

Sparkle_Kitty: He apparently threatened to kill his teacher

Sparkle_Kitty: (he really scares me. I know he watches while I sleep)

DarkThunder92: …….

Sparkle_Kitty: ?

DarkThunder92: I don't know what to say to help hun,

DarkThunder92: (tbh he kinda scares me too)

Unknown Prey: Who?

DarkThunder92: Shut up Unknown, This don't concern you

Unknown Prey: >.<

Dark Thunder92: So…When does he get out ?

Dark Thunder92: ?

Dark Thunder92:-waves hands in front of face-

Dark Thunder92: Sparkle?

Dark Thunder92: Hello….

DarkThunder92: -pokes- are you there?

Unknown Prey: She is busy

DarkThunder92: Shut up Unknown, how would you know?

Unknown Prey: Cause I have her head dangling from my hands

DarkThunder92:WTF!

DarkThunder92: You are a creepy person unknown, FUCKIN LEAVE!

Unknown Prey92: What's a matter Richard? Can you not boot me out of the room?

Unknown Prey92: That's right, only Alice can

DarkThunder92: How the hell did you know my name?

Unknown Prey92: I know a lot of things Richard. Like how you are reaching under your bed, digging for your cell phone right now.

Unknown Prey92: I see your stupid Star Wars sheets and know exactly what you're gonna do

DarkThunder92: Go to hell you psyco stalker

Unknown Prey92: Stalkers are weak, they prey on innocent people they barely know

Unknown Prey92: I am more of a maniac, I prefer to let people know who I am before I kill them

DarkThunder92: I'm reporting you to the mod right now freak

Unknown Prey92: Go ahead, You will be logging off soon anyway

DarkThunder92: What makes you so sure?

Unknown Prey92: Because I watched you call Alice's phone. I heard it ring on her dead body

Unknown Prey92: Now you are digging for your keys, you are going to try to drive that Camaro of yours over to her house

DarkThunder92: You are really scaring me, please quit it

Unknown Prey: oh, one last thing before you log off Richard

DarkThunder92: ?

Unknown Prey: They released me at 2:45 today

JohnJohn joined the chat

JohnJohn: Hello

Unknown Prey: hello John how are you?

JohnJohn: Im good and you?

Unknown Prey: Im doing well thank you

JohnJohn: hello Thunder, didn't think you would be on today

Unknown Prey: oh he won't answer you

JohnJohn: oh? Is he brb?

Unknown Prey: not exactly

JohnJohn: okay im confused

Unknown Prey: he's dead, I have his head dangling from my hands

JohnJohn: haha very funny, you are creepy as hell you know that.

Unknown Prey: You have no idea Johnathan Isaac Pierce

JohnJohn has left the chat

Admission

HR Toye

The little man climbed to the top of the platform. His flashy red suspenders and jaunty yellow carnation, followed by the booming chant, easily captured the attention of the crowd. "Hurry, hurry, hurry! Step right up for the greatest show of your lives! You, Sir" he pointed at a man in the front row of the crowd.

The man looked to his left and right, and silently mouthed, "Me?"

"Yes, you Sir. Come on up here." The young man, filled with trepidation ascended the stairs to the platform. "Now, how would you like the chance to win a fabulous prize?"

"Umm…yeah, I guess so," the young man mumbled.

"Speak up Son; the people in back can't hear you. Now, I said would you like to win a fabulous prize?"

"Yes Sir, I would," he said a bit louder.

"What's your name, Son?"

"My name is D-Dennis," he stammered.

The little man used his right foot to flick a switch located on the floor of the platform, which activated a trap door. Up from the hidden door rose a box that stood six feet tall. In the center of the box was a red and white painted target. The middle of the target had a shiny black button. The crowd stood in silence, waiting in anticipation.

The little man walked to the back of the box and opened a small door. He reached in grabbing a basket that contained three baseballs. He carried the basket to Dennis. He looked out, once again acknowledging the crowd. "Dennis here has three shots to hit the button with the ball. And…" he paused for effect, "he has a paltry distance of ten feet to do it. Do you think he can hit it?" The crowd cheered in response.

"Step back to that black X taped on the floor, Son." Dennis hadn't noticed it before. He walked to the spot and sat the basket on the floor. With one baseball in hand, he took aim and threw it towards the target. The crowd watched as his first attempt went far to the left and bounced off the box.

His second attempt went high by a couple of inches. He didn't know what the fabulous prize was; he just wanted to get the hell off the platform. He was starting to feel sick, he hated crowds. Worse, he hated being the person the crowd was staring at. He reached for the third ball, the flutters in his stomach intensified.

He threw the ball, and to his surprise, it hit its mark. A cheer came from the audience as a beacon light appeared at the top of the box. Red light pulsated making him feel even more nauseated. As the light disappeared, a mechanical voice proclaimed, "Winner, winner." This was followed by a loud clicking. The crowd leaned in to see what the prize was.

The clicking was being made by the target as it rose. Dennis leaned forward, straining his eyes to see what was beneath the target. His eyes widened in terror and his mouth made an O of shocked surprise as the ball of fire hit him in the chest.

The flames licked greedily at his clothes and skin. Next, his hair ignited. Dennis spun around and dropped to the ground, rolling back and forth trying to extinguish the fire. His body jerked spasmodically, as if doing a macabre break dance. The screams that ripped from his throat died away to a gurgle; soon the only sound to be heard was the sizzling of his flesh.

The fire did not spread to the platform; rather it seemed only to consume what was left of Dennis. It soon burned out, leaving nothing but ash and charred bones to remind others that a man had been there. A gentle breeze caught the ash and spread it over the audience. The crowd stood in morbid fascination. The spectacle did not seem to be over however, the bones began to move; not from the wind, but seemingly of their own accord.

They stood upright, reassembling themselves, much to the amusement of the crowd. They began to clap at the unusual trick. Once reformed, flesh began to grow over the bones. Skin and hair reappeared, gradually filling out to once again make the body of Dennis.

"I never get tired of that," the little man said to the dazed Dennis. "You won! Go and take your place in the crowd." Dennis nodded but said nothing as he dismounted the platform and went to stand at the front of the group. The little man laughed; it was a shrill cackling sound that hinted of insanity.

"The next show starts in thirty minutes," he proclaimed as he took a deep bow. He jumped down with a practiced movement and headed for the exit of the tent. He walked along the breezeway towards the exit. He observed the wall that surrounded the area for a moment before walking towards the ticket booth. He knocked on the glass until he gained the attention of the woman inside.

She looked at the creepy little man and said, "We have a big crowd tonight."

He peered through the opening to observe the people that stood behind the wall. "Yes, look at them, milling around confused. They look like cows waiting to be slaughtered." He laughed at his own joke until tears formed at the edges of his eyes. "Well, shall I herd them in?"

He exited through the turnstile and assessed the crowd. He bellowed out to them, "Tickets, get your tickets right here. Ladies and Gentlemen…have you wondered why you are here? The answers lie inside." The crowd haphazardly formed a line to the ticket booth.

"One at a time now, that's right. Get your ticket and go through the turnstile. Hurry, hurry, hurry. Step right up for the biggest event of your lives! One little ticket is all it takes. You just need to get you tickets for admission!"

*****

The crowd thinned as each one received their ticket and pushed through the turnstile. The little man watched as Dennis made his way up the line. Just as Dennis approached the ticket booth, he was able to make his move. "You," he thrust his index finger forward, poking Dennis hard in the chest.

Dennis' eyes widen in shock, not only because it felt like the finger was about to go through his sternum, but also because what remained of the crowd now had their eyes on him. He felt as if he had become paralyzed not even able to take a step backward from the invading finger. "You don't belong here," grinned the little man. Using his free hand he motioned towards the rest of the crowd. He leaned forward so that only Dennis could hear his next words.

Dennis felt the acrid breath hit is face, even though the man was at least a foot and a half shorter. His blood ran cold at the whispered words. "They have their own Hell to get to, yours is back at the tent." Dennis let loose a shrill laugh, one that bordered on insanity. He wondered how long it would be before he finally cracked, not much longer now. He hurried back to his tent; after all, there was another show in fifteen minutes.

Delightful

H.R. Toye

Amelia could feel the eyes of her classmates bore into her as the teacher called her name. Why did that stupid Mrs. Peterson make them read their poetry assignments out loud anyway? The students turned their heads to watch Amelia's slow progress as she made her way to the front of the room. Her pigtails bounced in time with each step she took.

"We're waiting, Miss Nichols," Mrs. Peterson addressed Amelia. Several students chuckled in response as Amelia glared at her teacher. Finally she reached her destination. She smoothed her pleated blue skirt and stared at the scuffs on her tennis shoes as she tried to calm the butterflies in her stomach. She could feel her cheeks burning with embarrassment as thirty-four pairs of eyes burned into her from their safe positions behind wooden desks.

Two fifth grade classes along with some of their parents were in attendance for the poetry reading. It was worth a regular grade plus a test grade. She looked at the audience noting that neither one of her parents were among the others standing at the back. But that was to be expected. Her father had left two years ago and Mommy...

She let the thought drift away as she looked at the poem clutched in her sweating hands.

Amelia cleared her throat and took a deep breath. She took a couple of swallows of air, trying to force her stomach to settle back into its proper position. She knows the longer she stands here without saying anything, the lower her grade will be. Mrs. Peterson is not known for her patience.

"M-m-my poem is t-titled Delightful," she stammered. She looked around the room for support, none was offered.

"Come on," someone called from the back row. She couldn't tell who it was, but she thought it might be that jerk Bobby Miller. He was always pulling her hair at recess and teasing her because her family wasn't as rich as his was. She cast an evil look in the general direction the interruption came from.

She started again, "My poem is titled Delightful." She plunged ahead, now fueled by anger.

"With dark curling hair

And big blue eyes,

An intense look that can mesmerize

Mommy says I'm delightful.

"I want a doll

From the store.

'She says no, I don't need more.'

I throw a tantrum to be spiteful.

"We get in the car

And leave for home.

We are all alone.

Mommy said, 'Cake would be delightful.'

"I grab the knife

From the table.

She looks at me like I'm unstable.

A glance at Mommy shows that she is frightful.

"'I wanted the doll!'

I yell as I stab.

Her screaming stops as I slice and jab.

Bathing in her blood was delightful."

Amelia finished the poem and waited for the applause that is initiated by Mrs. Peterson after all the poetry readings, but none came. She raised her head and looked at the shocked faces of the audience. Some of the faces looked mad; others were slack-jawed with eyes slightly bulging. No one was congratulating her on her poem. She looked to her teacher for help. But Mrs. Peterson wasn't looking at her. She had her arms crossed over her ample chest and was speaking with the teacher's aide Ms. Newman in a lowered voice. She tried, but couldn't make out what the two were saying.

Now, angrier than ever, Amelia crumpled the paper between clenched fists. She began to walk back to her desk and heard the words "now" and "go" uttered from behind her. She chose to ignore the voices and continued to her seat. A startled cry escaped her lips as she was grabbed on either side by the teacher and her aide.

"What..."

"Not another word, young lady," she was abruptly cut off by Mrs. Peterson. Ms. Newman pried her fingers open and confiscated the poem.

She was ushered into the hallway. Amelia was furious by the way she was being treated. She wrote the damn poem, didn't she? She blushed slightly at using her   Mommy's favorite explicit. She instantly admonished herself; she hadn't said it out loud. She even read the stupid thing like they wanted her to. Why was everyone acting so mad at her?

She was forced to sit outside the principal's office in one of the plastic chairs reserved for the "bad kids". She could hear the hushed sounds of the teacher speaking with the principal, Mr. Davidson. She couldn't hear what was being said but she was sure they were discussing her poem. Otherwise, why would she be dragged to the office right after reading it, she wondered?

She busied herself with kicking her feet against the metal legs of the chair. The grey-haired Ms. Jenkins glared at Amelia over the top of her glasses. Amelia couldn't stand the school's receptionist. She smelled like mothballs and old person and wore too much make-up. Amelia figured she was trying to look younger, but the make-up caked in the wrinkles just made her look older in her opinion. She kicked the legs of the chair harder just to annoy the old woman.

Mr. Davidson opened the door and nodded at Ms. Jenkins. "You can go in now," Ms. Jenkins announced with a falsely sweet smile that revealed yellowed and cracked teeth. Amelia wondered why he didn't just say so, I'm right here. She got up after kicking the legs a final time. She smiled at the resulting metallic ding that echoed through the office. The smile widened at Ms. Jenkins ensuing glare.

She followed Mr. Davidson into the office and sat in the one vacant chair in the room. All the adults' attention was on her. This was not going to be good. Mr. Davidson sat in his chair and rested his chin on tented fingers. He inhaled deeply; his gaze fixed on a point somewhere above her head. As he exhaled, his eyes finally met Amelia's.

"Miss Nichols..." he held up a hand as Amelia opened her mouth to talk. She shut it with an audible click. "In light of what your teacher has told me," he resumed as if there had been no interruption, "I think we are going to have to call your mother."

"But..." again she was silenced by the hand.

"Mrs. Peterson and I have agreed that your poem is going to receive an F. I don't know what you were thinking Miss Nichols. You have upset many of your classmates and the visiting parents. This is not the kind of image we want them to have of this school. Also..." he sighed for effect, "you will be writing a formal letter of apology to Mrs. Peterson and a copy will be sent home with each of the students."

Her cheeks flamed with anger and she could feel a vein at her left temple begin to throb. She stood so violently that her chair fell over with a resounding clatter. "That's not fair," she screamed.

"Young lady, control yourself!"

"I wrote the damn poem," she shrieked, now unashamed at using the curse word.

"I want you to go and have a chat with the counselor, Ms. Mason, while we are trying to get a hold of your mother." He said through gritted teeth. With that, Amelia was dismissed and escorted away by Ms. Newman.

Ms. Newman kept her hand firmly on Amelia's shoulder. "Why is everyone so mad at me?" She asked the aide as she was being led down the hall. She looked up at the usually friendly woman and   waited. Ms. Newman didn't say a word in response to the child, she just kept walking. She didn't even falter in her stride.

They approached the door to the counselor's office moments later. Ms. Newman knocked on the door and waited for admittance. When the knock was answered by the counselor she uttered a simple, "Wait here," then went inside to speak with Ms. Mason. Amelia leaned against the wall next to the door and waited for the two women to return. Five minutes later Ms. Newman exited the office. She turned to face Amelia and motioned her through the open door.

Amelia inched her way into the office. She was greeted by the concerned face of Ms. Mason. "Have a seat Amelia."

Amelia complied and sat in the chair that was slightly more comfortable than the one she had occupied in the principal's office. The butterfly feeling had returned to her stomach. The woman was looking at her as if she was expecting something. Amelia didn't know what she wanted. After a couple of minutes passed with neither one talking Amelia couldn't take it anymore. "What?" She shouted.

"There is no need to yell young lady." Ms. Mason admonished. "Let's just have a talk."

"Everyone is being so mean to me," Amelia sulked.

"And why do you think that is?

"I don't know, I just read my stupid poem."

"Ah... your poem. What is it about your poem that you think may have upset your teacher and your classmates?"

"I don't know."

"Okay, Amelia. How about we talk about something else for a while. What is your favorite toy?" Ms. Mason listened thoughtfully as Amelia began to discuss at length her collection of dolls. The child seemed relieved at the change of topic. The counselor made notes on a yellow legal pad occasionally.

The subject was switched several times in the half hour the child was in the office. Ms. Mason was careful to avoid the subject of the poem and of her mother which seemed to agitate the child every time she was brought up. "Why don't you have a piece of candy?" She proffered Amelia the glass jar full of hard candy and bubble gum that sat on the edge of her desk. Amelia selected a butterscotch disc. After unwrapping it she popped it into her mouth and dropped the plastic into the trash receptacle to the left of the desk.

"Thanks."

"You're welcome. I need to go and check on something, I'll be right back."

"Okay," She beamed. Ms. Mason was again amazed by the effect a piece of candy can have on a child.

Ms. Mason walked to the front office. After greeting Ms. Jenkins, she stepped through the principal's open door. "Harold?" She noticed the disturbed look on his face. "Have you been able to contact Amelia's mother?" She observed that the aide was not in the room, but the grim-faced Mrs. Peterson still occupied a chair at the corner.

"No, we haven't. I tried her work and it seems that she has not been in for the last two days. She hasn't even called in."

"Maybe she has been sick. Have you tried her at home?"

"Yes, we've called twice and there is no answer there either."

"Amelia seems very distressed any time the subject of her mother is brought up. Maybe someone should go by her house and check?" She ventured.

"An excellent idea," Mr. Davidson seemed relieved. "Mrs. Peterson, why don't you retrieve Amelia from Ms. Mason's office and take her into the library? Ms. Mason, check back in with me as soon as you've gone to Mrs. Nichols' house.

"Oh, but that's..." Mr. Davidson raised questioning brows and Ms. Mason knew it was useless to argue. "I'll call you after I get there." She walked back into the front office and rolled her eyes.

"He's good at that," Ms. Jenkins remarked. She handed over a piece of paper with an address scrawled on it. The two women shared a chuckle at the ingenuity of the principal. Ms. Mason grabbed her purse from the teacher's lounge and headed for her car.

She turned her air on full blast to combat the unseasonably warm April day. She smirked as the tinny voice of the weatherman announced that it was going to be another scorcher. "No shit," she said to the radio. The weather report was followed by the tune of a familiar song that she hummed along with.

Fifteen minutes later Ms. Mason was pulling her car into the driveway of the Nichols' house. It was like any other suburban home in the neighborhood, a brick one-level with a carport. The carport currently housed a newish Buick. It would appear that Amelia's mother was home.

As she knocked the door inched open. Ms. Mason called out, "Mrs. Nichols, are you home? This is Ms. Mason from your daughter's school."

After waiting a couple of minutes she tried again. "Mrs. Nichols, are you there?" She thought about turning around, going back to her car, and then calling Harold to let him know that Mrs. Nichols wasn't home.

Then she remembered the car sitting under the carport. If she's not there, then she will never know that I was here, she rationalized. But, if she's really sick she may need some help. Ms. Mason debated with herself for another minute, then stepped over the threshold.

She looked around the living room. She noted a hallway opened up off of the left and decided to check through there first. There were two doors on the left and three doors on the right. The two doors on the left were both bedrooms, one looked like Amelia's and the other looked as though it was being used as an office. The first door she tried on the right was a bathroom.

She began to feel a bit bad about the invasion of privacy she was causing, but she continued. The next door turned out to be a linen closet. The last room on the right was the master bedroom; it too was   empty. She decided she needed to leave. This was wrong, she shouldn't be here going through someone's house when they're obviously not home. Worse, it was a student's home. What if Mrs. Nichol's came home and decided to sue the school?

She was just about to the front door when a smell caught her attention. It wasn't overwhelming, it was just a whiff. It stopped her dead in her tracks. She crossed the living room and headed towards the kitchen. The smell was much stronger. The sickly sweet odor of something dead and rotting reached her nostrils, making her gorge rise. She coughed and put a hand over her nose. Ms. Mason tried to breathe through her mouth but the smell became overpowering as she breached the doorway.

The kitchen had a doorway leading off to the left and one to the right. One was probably the dining room, the other a utility room. The smell was definitely coming from the right. Stop! I should stop right now and call the police the small voice at the back of her mind screamed. But the curiosity was too strong.

She went through the entryway. The room was dimly lit. She noticed heavy drapes covered the windows and only small shafts of light managed to peek through on either side of the window dressings. She took a step into the room feeling for a light switch. Another step brought her crashing down on top of the source of malodorous object.

A scream ripped from her throat as her hand sank deep into the gelatinous flesh of the rotting Mrs. Nichols. Ms. Mason hastily stood and wiped her hand repeatedly on the leg of her slacks. She tried to block from her mind the way her hand had slid into what she was afraid was a wound on the woman's upper thigh. Congealed bits of blood were clinging to her fingernails.

She had dropped her purse when she fell and the contents were strewn both around and on the body. Careful to avoid the corpse, she felt on the wall again for the light. Luckily, she found the switch and illumination flooded the room. The phone, she had to find her cell phone. She held her breath as she plucked the phone off of the woman's blood covered blouse. She managed to punch the numbers 9-1-1, but was unable to speak when prompted by the emergency dispatcher.

"911, what is your emergency?" The disembodied voice floated up to her as she dropped the phone. The cell phone hit the tile and echoed like a gunshot in the quiet of the house. Her vision began to grey. She managed to take three lumbering steps back into the kitchen before she lost consciousness.

*****

The sirens cut through the stillness of the neighborhood as the ambulance and police car approached the house. Ms. Mason was taken away by the ambulance and treated for shock. Soon after their departure the coroner was called. The cause of death was determined to be a stab wound to the neck, where Amelia had severed her Mother's Jugular vein. The coroner counted at least fifty-seven stab wounds. There were no hesitation marks.

When the police questioned Amelia about her Mother's death, she smiled and said "Mommy thinks I am delightful." Soon after her detainment, she regressed to the speech patterns of a five year old and acted as one. She was admitted to a children's mental facility where she will remain until her eighteenth birthday.

The police searched Amelia's room and found a journal. The journal had several entries over the last two years detailing the deaths of two of her classmates and several neighborhood pets. The first entry was a poem titled "Princess". It reads as follows:

Daddy says he loves me best

I am his little princess

Mommy's like a wicked witch

He calls her a worthless bitch

He told me goodbye

He said do not cry

I didn't want him to go

I told him no!

Daddy always loved me best

I was his little princess

I gave him mommy's sleeping pills

I didn't know it was going to kill

www.ingramcontent.com/pod-product-compliance
Lightning Source LLC
Chambersburg PA
CBHW071232130626
46556CB00003B/978